A MAN FROM THE NORTH

Arnold Bennett

A Man from the North

ALAN SUTTON PUBLISHING LIMITED

First published in 1898

First published in this edition in the United Kingdom in 1994
Alan Sutton Publishing Limited
Phoenix Mill · Far Thrupp · Stroud · Gloucestershire

First published in this edition in the United States of America in 1994
Alan Sutton Publishing Inc.
83 Washington Street · Dover · NH 03820

British Library Cataloguing-in-Publication Data

A catalogue record for this book is available from the British Library.

ISBN 0-7509-0667-7

Library of Congress Catalogung-in-Publication Data applied for.

Cover picture: detail from The Flower Seller *by William Powell Frith (Guildhall Art Gallery, London;
photograph: The Bridgeman Art Library)*

Typset in 10/11 Bembo.
Typesetting and origination by
Alan Sutton Publishing Limited.
Printed in Great Britain by
The Guernsey Press Company Ltd,
Guernsey, Channel Islands.

TO THE ONE
WHOM I MOST HONOUR

BIOGRAPHICAL NOTE

ARNOLD BENNETT (1867–1931) was a successful, prolific and versatile writer, now best known as a novelist whose major works introduced the mainstream of European realism to early twentieth-century English Literature. He presented the seamy side of provincial life, dispassionately recording its ugly and sordid features, sometimes ironically and always without censure, in a series of over thirty novels and collections of short stories. Yet he was the author of more than seventy books in all, a cosmopolitan and industrious journalist who performed at many levels of seriousness, a perceptive critic of contemporary music, literature and art, as well as a playwright and essayist who became a popular figure in the early twentieth-century literary establishment.

(Enoch) Arnold Bennett was born on 27 May 1867 at Hanley, Staffordshire, one of the 'Five Towns' (properly six) of the Potteries now comprising Stoke-on-Trent. The eldest of six children of a self-made Methodist provincial solicitor (who had also been a schoolmaster), he was brought up in an atmosphere of sturdy middle-class respectability and self-improvement of an uncommonly cultured and bookish household. He was educated at the Burslem Endowed School and the Middle School at Newcastle-under-Lyme, later attending a local art school (he painted charming watercolours to the end of his life). At the age of eighteen he worked as a clerk in his father's office, where he contributed precocious weekly articles to a local newspaper.

He left the Potteries in 1889 for London where, after a period articled to a firm of solicitors, he soon put aside his law studies and laboured to establish himself in journalism. He wrote popular and sensational serial fiction, becoming assistant editor (1894), and later editor (1896–1900), of a women's magazine, *Woman*, where he wrote on a variety of topics from society gossip, fashion and recipes to book and, above all, theatre reviews. His writing was increasingly in demand from other magazines, including the leading critical journal *Academy*, and the popular press. Encouraged by the publication of a short story in the fashionable *Yellow Book* in July 1895, he embarked on a first novel, which was published in 1898 as *A Man from the North*.

In 1900 he resigned his editorship of *Woman* to become a professional writer, continuing to contribute freelance short stories and serial novels to magazines. *The Grand Babylon Hotel* (1902), a sensational and popular work in the manner of Ouida, was published in the same year as *Anna of the Five Towns* (1902), a work of serious literary pretensions under the influence of George Moore and Émile Zola. This is now considered one of his best novels, describing against the fictional background of the Five Towns of the Staffordshire Potteries a heroine of honesty and compassion who refuses to compromise with provincial Methodist society.

In 1903, after his father's death, he moved from a farmhouse in the Bedfordshire countryside to metropolitan Paris, in the footsteps of the artists and writers whom he most admired. In Paris he conceived his greatest and best known novel, *The Old Wives' Tale* (1908), which established, and has since largely maintained, his reputation. This is a novel of finely drawn characters set against a vividly realized background: the heroines are two sisters, one allegedly inspired by an ungainly elderly woman whom he had seen in a Paris restaurant in 1903. When the *Clayhanger* trilogy appeared (1910–1916; reprinted 1925 as *The Clayhanger Family*), his stature as one of the leading serious novelists of the day was confirmed. Showing him as a meticulous and often comic dramatist and historian of life in the Five Towns, it concerns the gloomy life of Edwin Clayhanger and his desperate love for Hilda Lessways and, in the final volume, their life together.

In Paris, Bennett wrested free of his provincial attitudes, becoming a cosmopolitan inhabitant of the Paris of the end of the *belle époque*, a melting-pot of artistic and literary influences and experiment. An early admirer of the French masters, he had been among the first English novelists to learn from studying the technique of Balzac, Flaubert, the de Goncourts, de Maupassant and Zola, and his criticism is of a high order; it demonstrates his early appreciation of the contemporary arts, of the Post-impressionist painters, of the ballet of Diaghilev and Stravinsky, as well as of the young writers, including Joyce, D.H. Lawrence and Faulkner. In 1907 he married a French actress, Marguerite Soulié, from whom he was separated in 1921.

When, after ten years in Paris, Bennett returned to England, he was a figure of the literary establishment, rich beyond the dreams of most authors, and offered a knighthood (in 1918; which he declined). He divided his time between London, Paris, a yacht and a country house in Essex, never returning to the Potteries except for brief visits, although they were to continue to provide the imaginative background to his novels. He wrote with remarkable facility, publishing novels and short stories, working as a journalist (particularly a powerful propagandist, during the War years, and before them in A.R. Orage's brilliant journal, *New Age*) and writing a number of plays. The latter include *Milestones* (1912; with E. Knoblock) and *The Great Adventure* (1913; adapted from an earlier novel), which were popular successes.

A precursor of modernism who owed much to the example of the European realist, his reputation suffered a decline after the great novels of the pre-war years: the modernists condemned his technique as providing mere 'photography', for its excessively scientific and unstructured accumulation of details. From this it was retrieved by the publication in 1923 of *Riceyman Steps*, the last of his major novels and a popular and critical success. It is a brilliant achievement in technique and design, set in the dark and squalid suburbs of London. The sinister tale concerns a miserly second-hand-book dealer who starves himself to death and whose contagious passion for thrift dominates his household, with terrible consequences for his wife. Here Bennett's handling of atmosphere, his psychological observation and kindly tolerance of feeling contribute to a final masterpiece.

In 1924 Arnold Bennett was moved to complete the novella *Elsie and the Child − A Tale of Riceyman Steps* reintroducing Elsie from the original novel, now working with her husband Joe in the household of Dr Raste.

The Journals of Arnold Bennett 1896–1928, a fascinating account of his life and times, were edited by Newman Flower (3 vols., 1932–3) after his death of typhoid fever in Marylebone, London, on 27 March 1931.

NICHOLAS MANDER

I

There grows in the North Country a certain kind of youth of whom it may be said that he is born to be a Londoner. The metropolis, and everything that appertains to it, that comes down from it, that goes up into it, has for him an imperious fascination. Long before schooldays are over he learns to take a doleful pleasure in watching the exit of the London train from the railway station. He stands by the hot engine and envies the very stoker. Gazing curiously into the carriages, he wonders that men and women who in a few hours will be treading streets called Piccadilly and the Strand can contemplate the immediate future with so much apparent calmness; some of them even have the audacity to look bored. He finds it difficult to keep from throwing himself in the guard's van as it glides past him; and not until the last coach is a speck upon the distance does he turn away and, nodding absently to the ticket-clerk, who knows him well, go home to nurse a vague ambition and dream of Town.

London is the place where newspapers are issued, books written, and plays performed. And this youth, who now sits in an office, reads all the newspapers. He knows exactly when a new work by a famous author should appear, and awaits the reviews with impatience. He can tell you off-hand the names of the pieces in the bills of the twenty principal West-end theatres, what their quality is, and how long they may be expected to run; and on the production of a new play, the articles of the dramatic critics provide him with sensations almost as vivid as those of the most zealous first-nighter at the performance itself.

Sooner or later, perhaps by painful roads, he reaches the goal of his desire. London accepts him – on probation; and as his strength is, so she demeans herself. Let him be bold and resolute, and she will make an obeisance, but her heel is all too ready to crush the coward and hesitant; and her victims, once underfoot, do not often rise again.

II

The antique four-wheeler, top-heavy with luggage, swung unsteadily round by Tattersall's and into Raphael Street. Richard thrust down the window with a sharp bang, indicative of a strange new sense of power; but before the cab came to a standstill he had collected himself, and managed to alight with considerable decorum. When the door opened in answer to his second ring, a faint, sour odour escaped from the house, and he remembered the friendly feminine warnings which he had received at Bursley on the subject of London lodgings. The aspect of the landlady, however, reassured him; she was a diminutive old woman in ridiculously short skirts, with a yellow, crinkled face, grey eyes, and a warm, benevolent smile that conquered. As she greeted Richard she blushed like a girl, and made a little old-fashioned curtsey. Richard offered his hand, and, after wiping hers on a clean apron, she took it timidly.

'I hope we shall get on well together, sir,' she said, looking straight up into her new lodger's eyes.

'I'm sure we shall,' answered Richard, sincerely.

She preceded him up the narrow, frowsy staircase, which was full of surprising turns.

'You'll find these stairs a bit awkward at first,' she apologised. 'I've often thought of getting a bit of nice carpet on them, but what's the use? It would be done for in a week. Now, here's your room, sir, first floor front, with two nice French windows, you see, and a nice balcony. Now, about tidying it of a morning, sir. If you'll step out for a walk as soon as you get up, my daughter shall make the bed, and dust, and you'll come in and find it all nice and straight for breakfast.'

'Very well,' assented Richard.

'That's how I generally arrange with my young men. I like them to have their breakfast in a nice tidy room, you see, sir. Now, what will you have for tea, sir? A little nice bread and butter . . .'

When she was gone Richard formally surveyed his quarters: a long, rather low room, its length cut by the two windows which were Mrs Rowbotham's particular pride; between the windows a table with a faded green cloth, and a small bed opposite; behind the door an artfully concealed washstand; the mantelpiece, painted mustard yellow, bore divers squat earthenware figures, and was surmounted by an oblong mirror framed in rosewood; over the mirror an illuminated text, 'Trust in Jesus,' and over the text an oleograph, in collision with the ceiling, entitled 'After the Battle of Culloden.' The walls were decorated with a pattern of giant pink roses; and here and there, hiding the roses, were hung photographs of persons in their Sunday clothes, and landscapes hand-painted in oil, depicting bridges, trees, water, and white sails in the distance. But the furnishing of the room caused Richard no uneasiness; in a few moments he had mentally arranged how to make the place habitable, and thenceforth he only saw what should and would be.

Tea was brought in by a girl whose face proclaimed her to be Mrs Rowbotham's daughter. At the sight of her Richard privately winked; he had read in books about landladies' daughters, but this one gave the lie to books; she was young, she was beautiful, and Richard would have sworn to her innocence. With an accession of boldness which surprised himself, he inquired her name.

'Lily, sir,' she said, blushing like her mother.

He cut the new, heavy bread, and poured out a cup of tea with the awkwardness of one unaccustomed to such work, and, having made space on the tray, set the evening paper against the sugar basin, and began to eat and read. Outside were two piano organs, children shouting, and a man uttering some monotonous unintelligible cry. It grew dark; Mrs Rowbotham came in with a lamp and cleared the table; Richard was looking through the window, and neither spoke. Presently he sat down. That being his first night in London, he had determined to spend it quietly *at home*. The piano organs and the children were still strident. A peculiar feeling of isolation momentarily overcame him, and the noises of the street seemed to recede. Then he went to the window again, and noticed that the children were dancing quite gracefully; it occurred to him that they might be ballet children. He picked up the paper and examined the theatrical advertisements, at first idly, but afterwards in detail.

With a long sigh, he took his hat and stick, and went very slowly downstairs. Mrs Rowbotham heard him fumbling with the catch of the front door.

'Are you going out, sir?'

'Only just for a walk,' said Richard, nonchalantly.

'Perhaps I'd better give you a latch-key?'

'Thanks.'

Another moment and he was in the delicious streets, going east.

III

Although he had visited London but once before, and then only for a few hours, he was not unfamiliar with the topography of the town, having frequently studied it in maps and an old copy of Kelly's directory.

He walked slowly up Park Side and through Piccadilly, picking out as he passed them the French Embassy, Hyde Park Corner, Apsley House, Park Lane, and Devonshire House. As he drank in the mingled glare and glamour of Piccadilly by night, – the remote stars, the high sombre trees, the vast, dazzling interiors of clubs, the sinuous, flickering lines of traffic, the radiant faces of women framed in hansoms, – he laughed the laugh of luxurious contemplation, acutely happy. At last, at last, he had come into his inheritance. London accepted him. He was hers; she his; and nothing should part them. Starvation in London would itself be bliss. But he had no intention of starving! Filled with great purposes, he straightened his back, and just then a morsel of mud thrown up from a bus-wheel splashed warm and gritty on his cheek. He wiped it off caressingly, with a smile.

Although it was Saturday night, and most of the shops were closed, an establishment where watches and trinkets of 'Anglo-Spanish' gold, superb in appearance and pillowed on green plush, were retailed at alluring prices, still threw a brilliant light on the pavement, and Richard crossed the road to inspect its wares. He turned away, but retraced his steps and entered the shop. An assistant politely inquired his wishes.

'I want one of those hunters you have in the window at 29/6,' said Richard, with a gruffness which must have been involuntary.

'Yes, sir. Here is one. We guarantee that the works are equal to the finest English lever.'

'I'll take it.' He put down the money.

'Thank you. Can I show you anything else?'

'Nothing, thanks,' still more gruffly.

'We have some excellent chains . . .'

'Nothing else, thanks.' And he walked out, putting his purchase in his pocket. A perfectly reliable gold watch, which he had worn for years, already lay there.

At Piccadilly Circus he loitered, and then crossed over and went along Coventry Street to Leicester Square. The immense façade of the Ottoman Theatre of Varieties, with its rows of illuminated windows and crescent moons set against the sky, rose before him, and the glory of it was intoxicating. It is not too much to say that the Ottoman held a stronger fascination for Richard than any other place in London. The British Museum, Fleet Street, and the Lyceum were magic names, but more magical than either was the name of the Ottoman. The Ottoman, on the rare occasions when it happened to be mentioned in Bursley, was a synonym for all the glittering vices of the metropolis. It stank in the nostrils of the London delegates who came down to speak at the annual meetings of the local Society for the Suppression of Vice. But how often had Richard, somnolent in chapel, mitigated the rigours of a long sermon by dreaming of an Ottoman ballet, – one of those voluptuous spectacles, all legs and white arms, which from time to time were described so ornately in the London daily papers.

The brass-barred swinging doors of the Grand Circle entrance were simultaneously opened for him by two human automata dressed exactly alike in long semi-military coats, a very tall man and a stunted boy. He advanced with what air of custom he could command, and after taking a ticket and traversing a heavily decorated corridor, encountered another pair of swinging doors; they opened, and a girl passed out, followed by a man who was talking to her vehemently in French. At the same moment a gust of distant music struck Richard's ear. As he climbed a broad, thick-piled flight of steps, the music became louder, and a clapping of hands could be heard. At the top of the steps hung a curtain of blue velvet; he pushed aside its stiff, heavy folds with difficulty, and entered the auditorium.

The smoke of a thousand cigarettes enveloped the furthest parts of the great interior in a thin bluish haze, which was dissipated as it reached the domed ceiling in the rays of a crystal chandelier. Far in front and a little below the level of the circle lay a line of footlights broken by the silhouette of the conductor's head. A diminutive, solitary figure in red and yellow stood in the centre of the huge stage; it was kissing its hands to the audience with a mincing, operatic gesture; presently it tripped off backwards, stopping at every third step to bow; the applause ceased, and the curtain fell slowly.

The broad, semicircular promenade which flanked the seats of the grand circle was filled with a well-dressed, well-fed crowd. The men talked and laughed, for the most part, in little knots, while in and out, steering their way easily and rapidly among these groups, moved the women: some with rouged cheeks, greasy vermilion lips, and enormous liquid eyes; others whose faces were innocent of cosmetics and showed pale under the electric light; but all with a peculiar, exaggerated swing of the body from the hips, and all surreptitiously regarding themselves in the mirrors which abounded on every glowing wall.

Richard stood aloof against a pillar. Near him were two men in evening dress conversing in tones which just rose above the general murmur of talk and the high, penetrating tinkle of glass from the bar behind the promenade.

'And what did she say then?' one of the pair asked smilingly. Richard strained his ear to listen.

'Well, *she* told *me*,' the other said, speaking with a dreamy drawl, while fingering his watch-chain absently and gazing down at the large diamond in his shirt, – '*she* told *me* that she said she'd do for him if he didn't fork out. But I don't believe her. You know, of course . . . There's Lottie . . .'

The band suddenly began to play, and after a few crashing bars the curtain went up for the ballet. The rich *coup d'œil* which presented itself provoked a burst of clapping from the floor of the house and the upper tiers, but to Richard's surprise no one in his proximity seemed to exhibit any interest in the entertainment. The two men still talked with their backs to the stage, the women continued to find a pathway between the groups, and from within the bar came the unabated murmur of voices and tinkle of glass.

Richard never took his dazed eyes from the stage. The moving pageant unrolled itself before him like a vision, rousing new sensations, tremors of strange desires. He was under a spell, and when at last the curtain descended to the monotonous roll of drums, he awoke to the fact that several people were watching him curiously. Blushing slightly, he went to a far corner of the promenade. At one of the little tables a woman sat alone. She held her head at an angle, and her laughing, lustrous eyes gleamed invitingly at Richard. Without quite intending to do so he hesitated in front of her, and she twittered a phrase ending in *chéri*.

He abruptly turned away. He would have been very glad to remain and say something clever, but his tongue refused its office, and his legs moved of themselves.

At midnight he found himself in Piccadilly Circus, unwilling to go home. He strolled leisurely back to Leicester Square. The front of the Ottoman was in darkness, and the square almost deserted.

IV

He walked home to Raphael Street. The house was dead, except for a pale light in his own room. At the top of the bare, creaking stairs he fumbled a moment for the handle of his door, and the regular sound of two distinct snores descended from an upper storey. He closed the door softly, locked it, and glanced round the room with some eagerness. The smell of the expiring lamp compelled him to unlatch both windows. He extinguished the lamp, and after lighting a couple of candles on the mantelpiece drew a chair to the fireplace and sat down to munch an apple. The thought occurred to him: 'This is my home – for how long?'

And then:

'Why the dickens didn't I say something to that girl?'

Between the candles on the mantelpiece was a photograph of his sister, which he had placed there before going out. He looked at it with a half smile, and murmured audibly several times:

'Why the dickens didn't I say something to that girl, with her *chéri?*'

The woman of the photograph seemed to be between thirty and forty years of age. She was fair, with a mild, serious face, and much wavy hair. The forehead was broad and smooth and white, the cheek-bones prominent, and the mouth somewhat large. The eyes were a very light grey; they met the gaze of the spectator with a curious timid defiance, as if to say, 'I am weak, but I can at least fight till I fall.' Underneath the eyes – the portrait was the work of an amateur, and consequently had not been robbed of all texture by retouching – a few crowsfeet could be seen.

As far back as Richard's memory went, he and Mary had lived together and alone in the small Red House which lay half a mile out of Bursley, on the Manchester road. At one time it had been rurally situated, creeping plants had clothed its red walls, and the bare patch behind it had been a garden; but the gradual development of a coal-producing district had covered the fields with smooth, mountainous heaps of grey refuse, and stunted or killed every tree in the neighbourhood. The house itself was undermined, and in spite of iron clamps had lost most of its rectangles, while the rent had dropped to fifteen pounds a year.

Mary was very much older than her brother, and she had always appeared to him exactly the mature woman of the photograph. Of his parents he knew nothing except what Mary had told him, which was little and vague, for she watchfully kept the subject at a distance.

She had supported herself and Richard in comfort by a medley of vocations, teaching the piano, collecting rents, and practising the art of millinery. They had few friends. The social circles of Bursley were centred in its churches and chapels; and though Mary attended the Wesleyan sanctuary with some regularity, she took small interest in prayer-meetings, class-meetings, bazaars, and all the other minor religious activities, thus neglecting opportunities for intercourse which might have proved agreeable. She had sent Richard to the Sunday-school; but when, at the age of fourteen, he protested that Sunday-school was 'awful rot,' she answered calmly, 'Don't go then;' and from that day his place in class was empty. Soon afterwards the boy cautiously insinuated that chapel belonged to the same category as Sunday-school, but the hint failed of its effect.

The ladies of the town called sometimes, generally upon business, and took afternoon tea. Once the vicar's wife, who wished to obtain musical tuition for her three youngest daughters at a nominal fee, came in and found Richard at a book on the hearthrug.

'Ah!' said she. 'Just like his father, is he not, Miss Larch?' Mary made no reply.

The house was full of books. Richard knew them all well by sight, but until he was sixteen he read only a select handful of volumes which had stood the test of years. Often he idly speculated as to the contents of some of the others, – 'Horatii Opera,' for instance: had that anything to do with theatres? – yet for some curious reason, which when he grew older he sought for in vain, he never troubled himself to look into them. Mary read a good deal, chiefly books and magazines fetched for her by Richard from the Free Library.

When he was about seventeen, a change came. He was aware dimly, and as if by instinct, that his sister's life in the early days had not been without its romance. Certainly there was something hidden between her and William Vernon, the science master at the Institute, for they were invariably at great pains to avoid each other. He sometimes wondered whether Mr Vernon was connected in any way with the melancholy which was never, even in her brightest moments, wholly absent from Mary's demeanour. One Sunday night – Richard had been keeping house – Mary, coming in late from chapel, threw her arms round his neck as he opened the door, and, dragging down his face to hers, kissed him hysterically again and again.

'Dicky, Dick,' she whispered, laughing and crying at the same time, 'something's happened. I'm almost an old woman, but something's happened!'

'I know,' said Richard, retreating hurriedly from her embrace. 'You're going to marry Mr Vernon.'

'But how could you tell?'

'Oh! I just guessed.'

'You don't mind, Dick, do you?'

'I! Mind!' Afraid lest his feelings should appear too plainly, he asked abruptly for supper.

Mary gave up her various callings, the wedding took place, and William Vernon came to live with them. It was then that Richard began to read more widely, and to form a definite project of going to London.

He could not fail to respect and like William. The life of the married pair seemed to him idyllic; the tender, furtive manifestations of affection which were constantly passing between Mary and her sedate, middle-aged husband touched him deeply, and at the thought of the fifteen irretrievable years during which some ridiculous misunderstanding had separated this loving couple, his eyes were not quite as dry as a youth could wish. But with it all he was uncomfortable. He felt himself an intruder upon holy privacies; if at meal-times husband and wife clasped hands round the corner of the table, he looked at his plate; if they smiled happily upon no discoverable provocation, he pretended not to notice the fact. They did not need him. Their hearts were full of kindness for every living thing, but unconsciously they stood aloof. He was driven in upon himself, and spent much of his time either in solitary walking or hidden in an apartment called the study.

He ordered magazines whose very names Mr Holt, the principal bookseller in Bursley, was unfamiliar with, and after the magazines came books of verse and novels enclosed in covers of mystic design, and printed in a style which Mr Holt, though secretly impressed, set down as eccentric. Mr Holt's shop performed the functions of a club for the dignitaries of the town; and since he took care that this esoteric literature was well displayed on the counter until called for, the young man's fame as *a great reader* soon spread, and Richard began to see that he was regarded as a curiosity of which Bursley need not be ashamed. His self-esteem, already fostered into lustiness by a number of facile school successes, became more marked, although he was wise enough to keep a great deal of it to himself.

One evening, after Mary and her husband had been talking quietly some while, Richard came into the sitting-room.

'I don't want any supper,' he said, 'I'm going for a bit of a walk.'

'Shall we tell him?' Mary asked, smiling, after he had left the room.

'Please yourself,' said William, also smiling.

'He talks a great deal about going to London. I hope he won't go till – after April; I think it would upset me.'

'You need not trouble, I think, my dear,' William answered. 'He talks about it, but he isn't gone yet.'

Mr Vernon was not quite pleased with Richard. He had obtained for him – being connected with the best people in the town – a position as shorthand and general clerk in a solicitor's office, and had learnt privately that though the youth was smart enough, he was scarcely making that progress which might have been expected. He lacked 'application.' William attributed this shortcoming to the excessive reading of verse and obscure novels.

April came, and, as Mr Vernon had foretold, Richard still remained in Bursley. But the older man was now too deeply absorbed in another matter to interest himself at all in Richard's movements, – a matter in which Richard himself exhibited a shy concern. Hour followed anxious hour, and at last was heard the faint, fretful cry of a child in the night. Then stillness. All that Richard ever saw was a coffin, and in it a dead child at a dead woman's feet.

Fifteen months later he was in London.

V

Mr Curpet, of the firm of Curpet and Smythe, whose name was painted in black and white on the dark green door, had told him that the office hours were from nine-thirty to six. The clock of the Law Courts was striking a quarter to ten. He hesitated a moment, and then seized the handle; but the door was fast, and he descended the two double flights of iron stairs into the quadrangle.

New Serjeant's Court was a large modern building of very red brick with terra-cotta facings, eight storeys high; but in spite of its faults of colour and its excessive height, ample wall spaces and temperate ornamentation gave it a dignity and comeliness sufficient to distinguish it from other buildings in the locality. In the centre of the court was an oval patch of brown earth, with a few trees whose pale-leaved tops, struggling towards sunlight, reached to the middle of the third storey. Round this plantation ran an immaculate roadway of wooden blocks, flanked by an equally immaculate asphalt footpath. The court possessed its own private lampposts, and these were wrought of iron in an antique design.

Men and boys, grave and unconsciously oppressed by the burden of the coming day, were continually appearing out of the gloom of the long tunnelled entrance and vanishing into one or other of the twelve doorways. Presently a carriage and pair drove in, and stopped opposite Richard. A big man of about fifty, with a sagacious red and blue face, jumped alertly out, followed by an attentive clerk carrying a blue sack. It seemed to Richard that he knew the features of the big man from portraits, and, following the pair up the staircase of No. 2, he discovered from the legend on the door through which they disappeared that he had been in the presence of Her Majesty's Attorney-General. Simultaneously with a misgiving as to his ability to reach the standard of clerical ability doubtless required by Messrs Curpet and Smythe, who did business cheek by jowl with an attorney-general and probably employed him, came an elevation of spirit as he darkly guessed what none can realise completely, that a man's future lies on his own knees, and on the knees of no gods whatsoever.

He continued his way upstairs, but Messrs Curpet and Smythe's portal was still locked. Looking down the well, he espied a boy crawling reluctantly and laboriously upward with a key in his hand which he dragged across the bannisters. In course of time the boy reached Messrs Curpet and Smythe's door, and opening it stepped neatly over a pile of letters which lay immediately within. Richard followed him.

'Oh! My name's Larch,' said Richard, as if had just occurred to him that the boy might be interested in the fact. 'Do you know which is my room?'

The boy conducted him along a dark passage with green doors on either side, to a room at the end. It was furnished mainly with two writing-tables and two armchairs; in one corner was a disused copying-press, in another an immense pile of reporters' note-books; on the mantelpiece, a tumbler, a duster, and a broken desk lamp.

'That's your seat,' said the boy, pointing to the larger table, and disappeared. Richard disposed of his coat and hat and sat down, trying to feel at ease and not succeeding.

At five minutes past ten a youth entered with the 'Times' under his arm. Richard waited for him to speak, but he merely stared and took off his overcoat. Then he said, –

'You've got my hook. If you don't mind, I'll put your things on this other one.'

'Certainly,' assented Richard.

The youth spread his back luxuriously to the empty fireplace and opened the 'Times,' when another and smaller boy put his head in at the door.

'Jenkins, Mr Alder wants the "Times." '

The youth silently handed over the advertisement pages which were lying on the table. In a minute the boy returned.

'Mr Alder says he wants the inside of the "Times." '

'Tell Mr Alder to go to hell, with my compliments.' The boy hesitated.

'Go on, now,' Jenkins insisted. The boy hung on the door-handle, smiling dubiously, and then went out.

'Here, wait a minute!' Jenkins called him back. 'Perhaps you'd better give it him. Take the damn thing away.'

A sound of hurried footsteps in the next room was succeeded by an imperious call for Jenkins, at which Jenkins slipped nimbly into his chair and untied a bundle of papers.

'Jenkins!' the call came again, with a touch of irritation in it, but Jenkins did not move. The door was thrust open.

'Oh! You are there, Jenkins. Just come in and take a letter down.' The tones were quite placid.

'Yes, Mr Smythe.'

'I never take any notice of Smythe's calls,' said Jenkins, when he returned. 'If he wants me, he must either ring or fetch me. If I once began it, I should be running in and out of his room all day, and I've quite enough to do without that.'

'Fidgety, eh?' Richard suggested.

'Fidgety's no word for it, *I* tell you. Alder – that's the manager, you know – said only yesterday that he has less trouble with forty Chancery actions of Curpet's than with one county-court case of Smythe's. I know I'd a jolly sight sooner write forty of Curpet's letters than ten of Smythe's. I wish I'd got your place, and you'd got mine. I suppose you can write shorthand rather fast.'

'Middling,' said Richard. 'About 120.'

'Oh! We had a man once could do 150, but he'd been a newspaper reporter. I do a bit over a hundred, if I've not had much to drink overnight. Let's see, they're giving you twenty-five bob, aren't they?'

Richard nodded.

'The man before you had thirty-five, and he couldn't spell worth a brass button. I only get fifteen, although I've been here seven years. A damn shame I call it! But Curpet's beastly near. If he'd give some other people less, and me a bit more . . .'

'Who are "some other people"?' asked Richard, smiling.

'Well, there's old Aked. He sits in the outer office – you won't have seen him because he doesn't generally come till eleven. They give him a pound a week, just for doing a bit of engrossing when he feels inclined to engross, and for being idle when he feels inclined to be idle. He's a broken-down something or other, – used to be clerk to Curpet's father. He has some dibs of his own, and this just finds him amusement. I bet he doesn't do fifty folios a week. And he's got the devil's own temper.

Jenkins was proceeding to describe other members of the staff when the entry of Mr Curpet himself put an end to the recital. Mr Curpet was a small man, with a round face and a neatly trimmed beard.

'Good morning, Larch. If you'll kindly come into my room, I'll dictate my letters. Good morning, Jenkins.' He smiled and withdrew, leaving Richard excessively surprised at his suave courtesy.

In his own room Mr Curpet sat before a pile of letters, and motioned Richard to a side table.

'You will tell me if I go too fast,' he said, and began to dictate regularly, with scarcely a pause. The pile of letters gradually disappeared into a basket. Before half a dozen letters were done Richard comprehended that he had become part of a business machine of far greater magnitude than anything to which he had been accustomed in Bursley. This little man with the round face dealt impassively with tens of thousands of pounds; he mortgaged whole streets, bullied railway companies, and wrote familiarly with lords. In the middle of one long letter, a man came panting in, whom Richard at once took for Mr Alder, the Chancery manager. His rather battered silk hat was at the back of his head, and he looked distressed.

'I'm sorry to say we've lost that summons in Rice *v.* The L.R. Railway.'

'Really!' said Mr Curpet. 'Better appeal, and brief a leader, eh?'

'Can't appeal, Mr Curpet.'

'Well, we must make the best of it. Telegraph to the country. I'll write and keep them calm. It's a pity they were so sure. Rice will have to economise for a year or two. What was my last word, Larch?' The dictation proceeded.

One hour was allowed for lunch, and Richard spent the first moiety of it in viewing the ambrosial exteriors of Strand restaurants. With the exception of the coffee-house at Bursley, he had never been in a restaurant in his life, and he was timid of entering any of those sumptuous establishments whose swinging doors gave glimpses of richly decorated ceilings, gleaming tablecloths, and men in silk hats greedily consuming dishes placed before them by obsequious waiters.

At last, without quite knowing how he got there, he sat in a long, low apartment, papered like an attic bedroom, and odorous of tea and cake. The place was crowded with young men and women indifferently well-dressed, who bent over uncomfortably small oblong marble-topped tables. An increasing clatter of crockery filled the air. Waitresses, with pale, vacant faces, dressed in dingy black with white aprons, moved about with difficulty at varying rates of speed, but none of them seemed to betray an interest in Richard. Behind the counter, on which stood great polished urns emitting clouds of steam, were several women whose superior rank in the restaurant was denoted by a black apron, and after five minutes had elapsed Richard observed one of these damsels pointing out himself to a waitress, who approached and listened condescendingly to his order.

A thin man, rather more than middle-aged, with a grey beard and slightly red nose, entered and sat down opposite to Richard. Without preface he began, speaking rather fast and with an expressive vivacity rarely met with in the ageing, –

'Well, my young friend, how do you like your new place?'

Richard stared at him.

'Are you Mr Aked?'

'The same. I suppose Master Jenkins has made you acquainted with all my peculiarities of temper and temperament. – Glass of milk, roll, and two pats of butter – and, I say, my girl, try not to keep me waiting as long as you did yesterday.' There was a bright smile on his face, which the waitress unwillingly returned.

'Don't you know,' he went on, looking at Richard's plate, – 'don't you know that tea and ham together are frightfully indigestible?'

'I never have indigestion.'

'No matter. You soon will have if you eat tea and ham together. A young man should guard his digestion like his honour. Sounds funny, doesn't it? But it's right. An impaired digestive apparatus has ruined many a career. It ruined mine. You see before you, sir, what might have been an author of repute, but for a wayward stomach.'

'You write?' Richard asked, interested at once, but afraid lest Mr Aked might be cumbrously joking.

'I used to.' The old man spoke with proud self-consciousness.

'Have you written a book?'

'Not a book. But I've contributed to all manner of magazines and newspapers.'

'What magazines?'

'Well, let me see – it's so long ago. I've written for "Cornhill." I wrote for "Cornhill" when Thackeray edited it. I spoke to Carlyle once.'

'You did?'

'Yes. Carlyle said to me — Carlyle said to me — Carlyle said —' Mr Aked's voice dwindled to an inarticulate murmur, and, suddenly ignoring Richard's presence, he pulled a book from his pocket and began to finger the leaves. It was a French novel, 'La Vie de Bohème.' His face had lost all its mobile expressiveness.

A little alarmed by such eccentricity, and not quite sure that this associate of Carlyle was perfectly sane, Richard sat silent, waiting for events. Mr Aked was clearly accustomed to reading while he ate; he could even drink with his eyes on the book. At length he pushed his plates away from him, and closed the novel with a snap.

'I see you're from the country, Larch,' he said, as if there had been no lapse in the conversation. 'Now, why in God's name did you leave the country? Aren't there enough people in London?'

'Because *I* wanted to be an author,' answered Richard, with more assurance than veracity, though he spoke in good faith. The fact was that his aspirations, hitherto so vague as to elude analysis, seemed within the last few minutes mysteriously to have assumed definite form.

'You're a young fool,' then.'

'But I've an excellent digestion.'

'You won't have if you begin to write. Take my word, you're a young fool. You don't know what you're going in for, my little friend.'

'Was Murger a fool?' Richard said clumsily, determined to exhibit an acquaintance with 'La Vie de Bohème.'

'Ha! We read French, do we?'

Richard blushed. The old man got up.

'Come along,' he said peevishly. 'Let's get out of this hole.'

At the pay-desk, waiting for change, he spoke to the cashier, a thin girl with reddish-brown hair, who coughed, —

'Did you try those lozenges?'

'Oh! yes, thanks. They *taste* nice.'

'Beautiful day.'

'Yes; my word, isn't it!'

They walked back to the office in absolute silence; but just as they were going in, Mr Aked stopped, and took Richard by the coat.

'Have you anything special to do next Thursday night?'

'No,' said Richard.

'Well, I'll take you to a little French restaurant in Soho, and we'll have dinner. Half a crown. Can you afford?'

Richard nodded.

'And, I say, bring along some of your manuscripts, and I'll flay them alive for you.'

VI

An inconstant, unrefreshing breeze, sluggish with accumulated impurity, stirred the curtains, and every urban sound – high-pitched voices of children playing, roll of wheels and rhythmic trot of horses, shouts of newsboys and querulous barking of dogs – came through the open windows touched with a certain languorous quality that suggested a city fatigued, a city yearning for the moist recesses of woods, the disinfectant breath of mountain tops, and the cleansing sea.

On the little table between the windows lay pen, ink, and paper. Richard sat down to be an author. Since his conversation with Mr Aked of the day before he had lived in the full glow of an impulse to write. He discerned, or thought he discerned, in the fact that he possessed the literary gift, a key to his recent life. It explained, to be particular, the passion for reading which had overtaken him at seventeen, and his desire to come to London, the natural home of the author. Certainly it was strange that hitherto he had devoted very little serious thought to the subject of writing, but happily there were in existence sundry stray verses and prose fragments written at Bursley, and it contented him to recognise in these the first tremulous stirrings of a late-born ambition.

During the previous evening he had busied himself in deciding upon a topic. In a morning paper he had read an article entitled 'An Island of Sleep,' descriptive of Sark; it occurred to him that a similar essay upon Parchester, a comatose cathedral city which lay about thirty miles from Bursley, might suit a monthly magazine. He knew Parchester well; he had been accustomed to visit it from childhood; he loved it. As a theme full of picturesque opportunities it had quickened his imagination, until his brain seemed to surge with vague but beautiful fancies. In the night his sleep had been broken, and several new ideas had suggested themselves. And now, after a day of excited anticipation, the moment for composition had arrived.

As he dipped his pen in the ink a sudden apprehension of failure surprised him. He dismissed it, and wrote in a bold hand, rather carefully,–

MEMORIES OF A CITY OF SLEEP

That was surely an excellent title. He proceeded:–

On the old stone bridge, beneath which the clear, smooth waters of the river have crept at the same pace for centuries, stands a little child, alone. It is early morning, and the clock of the time-stained cathedral which lifts its noble gothic towers scarce a hundred yards away, strikes five, to the accompaniment of an unseen lark overhead.

He sat back to excogitate the next sentence, staring round the room as if he expected to find the words written on the wall. One of the gilt-framed photographs was slightly askew; he left his chair to put it straight; several other pictures seemed to need adjustment, and he levelled them all with scrupulous precision. The ornaments on the mantelpiece were not evenly balanced; these he rearranged entirely. Then, having first smoothed out a crease in the bedcover, he sat down again.

But most of the beautiful ideas which he had persuaded himself were firmly within his grasp now eluded him, or tardily presented themselves in a form so obscure as to be valueless, and the useful few that remained defied all attempts to bring them in to order. Dashed by his own impotence, he sought out the article on Sark, and examined it afresh. Certainly weekly organs of literature had educated him to sneer at the journalism of the daily press, but it appeared that the man who wrote 'An Island of Sleep' was at least capable of expressing himself with clearness and fluency, and possessed the skill to pass naturally from one aspect of his subject to another. It seemed simple enough. . . .

He went to the window.

The sky was a delicate amber, and Richard watched it change to rose, and from rose to light blue. The gas-lamps glared out in quick succession; some one lowered the blind of a window opposite his own, and presently a woman's profile was silhouetted against it for a moment, and then vanished. A melody came from the public house, sung in a raucous baritone to the thrumming of a guitar; the cries of the playing children had now ceased.

Suddenly turning into the room, he was astonished to find it almost in darkness; he could distinguish only the whiteness of the papers on the table.

He was not in the mood for writing to-night. Some men wrote best in the evening, others in the morning. Probably he belonged to the latter class. Be that as it might, he would rise at six the next morning and make a new beginning. 'It's only a question of practice, of course,' he said, half aloud, repressing a troublesome dubiety. He would take a short walk, and to early to bed. Gradually his self-confidence returned.

As he closed the front door there was a rustle of silks and a transient odour of violets; a woman had gone by. She turned slightly at the sound of the door, and Richard had a glimpse of a young and pretty face under a spreading hat, a full, ripe bust whose alluring contours were perfectly disclosed by a tight-fitting bodice, and two small white hands, in one a dangling pair of gloves, in the other an umbrella. He passed her, and waited at the corner by Tattersall's till she overtook him again. Now she stood on the kerb within six feet of him, humming an air and smiling to herself. Up went the umbrella to signal for a hansom.

'The Ottoman,' Richard heard her say across the roof of the cab, the driver leaning forward with his hand to his ear. What a child's voice it seemed, lisping and artless!

The cabman winked at Richard, and gently flicked his horse. In a moment the hansom was two dwindling specks of red in a shifting multitude of lights.

An hour later he saw her in the promenade of the theatre; she stood against a pillar, her eyes on the entrance. As their glances met, she threw her head a little backwards, like one who looks through spectacles on the end of his nose, and showed her teeth. He sat down near her.

Presently she waved her hand to a man who was coming in. He seemed about thirty, with small, clear eyes, bronzed cheeks, a heavy jaw, and a closely trimmed brown moustache. He was fashionably garbed, though not in evening dress, and he greeted her without raising his hat.

'Shall we have a drink?' she suggested. 'I'm so thirsty.'

'Fizz?' the man drawled. She nodded.

Soon they went out together, the man carelessly stuffing change for a five-pound note into his pocket.

'What's the difference between him and me?' Richard reflected as he walked home. 'But just wait a bit; wait till I've . . .' When he reached his lodgings the meanness of the room, of his clothes, of his supper, nauseated him. He dreamed that he was kissing the Ottoman girl, and that she lisped, 'Nice boy,' whereupon he cast a handful of sovereigns on her lap.

At six o'clock the next morning he was working at his article. In two days it was finished, and he had despatched it to a monthly magazine, 'together with a stamped directed envelope for its return if unsuitable,' in accordance with the editorial instructions printed below the table of contents in every number. The editor of the 'Trifler' promised that all manuscripts so submitted, and written on one side of the paper only, should be dealt with promptly.

He had been expecting to discuss his work with Mr Aked at the proposed dinner, but this had not taken place. On the morning after the arrangement had been made, Mr Aked fell ill, and in a few days he wrote to resign his post, saying that he had sufficient to live on, and felt 'too venerable for regular work.'

Richard held but the frailest hope that 'A City of Sleep' would be accepted, but when the third morning arrived, and the postman brought nothing, his opinion of the article began to rise. Perhaps it had merit, after all; he recalled certain parts of it which were distinctly clever and striking. Hurrying home from the office that afternoon, he met the landlady's daughter on the stairs, and said casually, –

'Any letters for me, Lily?'

'No, sir.' The girl had an attractive blush.

'I'll take a couple of eggs for tea, if Mrs Rowbotham has them.'

He remained at home in the evening, waiting for the last delivery, which occurred about 9.30. The double knocks of the postman were audible ten or twelve houses away. At last Richard heard him mounting the steps of No. 74, and then his curt rat-tat shook the house. A little thud on the bare wooden floor of the hall seemed to indicate a heavier package than the ordinary letter.

As, when a man is drowning, the bad actions of a whole lifetime present themselves to him in one awful flash, so at that moment all the faults, the hopeless crudities, of 'A City of Sleep' confronted Richard. He wondered at his own fatuity in imagining for a single instant that the article had the barest chance of acceptance. Was it not notorious that famous authors had written industriously for years without selling a line!

Lily came in with the supper-tray. She was smiling.

'Warm work, eh, Lily?' he said, scarcely knowing that he spoke.

'Yes, sir, it's that hot in the kitchen you wouldn't believe.' Setting down the tray, she handed him a foolscap envelope, and he saw his own handwriting as if in a dream.

'For me?' he murmured carelessly, and placed the letter on the mantelpiece. Lily took his orders for breakfast, and with a pleasant, timid 'Good night, sir,' left the room.

He opened the envelope. In the fold of his manuscript was a sheet of the best cream-laid notepaper bearing these words in flowing copperplate: 'The Editor presents his compliments to Mr Larch [written] and regrets to be unable to use the enclosed article, for the offer of which he is much obliged.'

The sight of this circular, with the offices of the magazine illustrated at the top, and the notification in the left-hand corner that all letters must be addressed to the editor and not to any member of the staff individually, in some mysterious way mitigated Richard's disappointment. Perhaps the comfort of it lay in the tangible assurance it afforded that he was now actually *a literary aspirant* and had communications, however mortifying, with *the press*.

He read the circular again and again during supper, and determined to re-write the article. But this resolve was not carried out. He could not bring himself even to glance through it, and finally it was sent to another magazine exactly as it stood.

Richard had determined to say nothing in the office about his writing until he could produce a printed article with his name at the foot; and frequently during the last few days his mouth had watered as he anticipated the sweetness of that triumph. But next day he could not refrain from showing to Jenkins the note from the 'Trifler.' Jenkins seemed impressed, especially when Richard requested him to treat the matter as confidential. A sort of friendship arose between them, and strengthened as time went on. Richard sometimes wondered how precisely it had come about, and why it continued.

VII

Albert Jenkins was nineteen years of age, and lived with his parents and seven brothers and sisters in Camberwell; his father managed a refreshment bar in Oxford Street. He had been in the employ of Messrs Curpet and Smythe for seven years, – first as a junior office boy, then as senior office boy, and finally as junior shorthand clerk. He was of the average height, with a shallow chest, and thin arms and legs. His feet were very small – he often referred to the fact with frank complacency – and were always encased in well-fitting hand-made boots, brightly polished. The rest of his attire was less remarkable for neatness; but at intervals an ambition to be genteel possessed him, and during these recurrent periods the nice conduct of his fingernails interfered somewhat with official routine. He carried his hat either at the back of his head or tilted almost upon the bridge of his nose. In the streets he generally walked with sedate deliberation, his hands deep in his pockets, his eyes lowered, and an enigmatic smile on his thin lips.

His countenance was of a pale yellow complexion just tinged with red, and he never coloured; his neck was a darker yellow. Upon the whole, his features were regular, except the mouth, which was large, and protruded like a monkey's; the eyes were grey, with a bold regard, which not seldom was excusably mistaken for insolence.

Considering his years, Jenkins was a highly accomplished person, in certain directions. Upon all matters connected with her Majesty's mail and inland revenue, upon cab fares, bus-routes, and local railways, upon 'Pitman outlines,' and upon chamber practice in Chancery, he was an unquestioned authority. He knew the addresses of several hundred London solicitors, the locality of nearly every street and square within the four-mile radius, and, within the same limits, the approximate distance of any one given spot from any other given spot.

He was the best billiard-player in the office, and had once made a spot-barred break of 49; this game was his sole pastime. He gambled regularly upon horse-races, resorting to a number of bookmakers, but neither winning nor losing to an appreciable extent; no less than three jockeys occasionally permitted him to enjoy their companionship, and he was never without a stable-tip.

His particular hobby, however, was restaurants. He spent half his income upon food, and quite half his waking hours either in deciding what he should consume, or in actual drinking and mastication. He had personally tested the merits of every bar and house of refreshment in the neighbourhood of the Law Courts, from Lockhart's to the Savoy, and would discourse for hours on their respective virtues and defects. No restaurant was too mean for his patronage, and none too splendid; for days in succession he would dine upon a glass of water and a captain biscuit with cheese, in order to accumulate resources for a delicate repast in one of the gilded establishments where the rich are wont to sustain themselves; and he had acquired from his father a quantity of curious lore, throwing light upon the secrets of the refreshment trade, which enabled him to spend the money thus painfully amassed to the best advantage.

Jenkins was a cockney and the descendant of cockneys; he conversed always volubly in the dialect of Camberwell; but just as he was subject to attacks of modishness, so at times he attempted to rid himself of his accent, of course without success. He swore habitually, and used no reticence whatever, except in the presence of his employers and of Mr Alder the manager. In quick and effective retort he was the peer of cabmen, and nothing could abash him. His favourite subjects of discussion were restaurants, as before mentioned, billiards, the turf, and women, whom he usually described as 'tarts.' It was his custom to refer to himself as a 'devil for girls,' and when Mr Alder playfully accused him of adventures with females of easy virtue, his delight was unbounded.

There were moments when Richard loathed Jenkins, when the gross and ribald atmosphere which attended Jenkins' presence nauseated him, and utter solitude in London seemed preferable to the boy's company; but these passed, and the intimacy throve. Jenkins, indeed, had his graces; he was of an exceedingly generous nature, and his admiration for the deep literary scholarship which he imagined Richard to possess was ingenuous and unconcealed. His own agile wit, his picturesque use of slang, his facility in new oaths, and above all his exact knowledge of the byways and backwaters of London life, endowed him, in Richard's unaccustomed eyes, with a certain specious attractiveness. Moreover, the fact that they shared the same room and performed similar duties made familiar intercourse between them natural and necessary. With no other member of the staff did Richard care to associate. The articled clerks, though courteously agreeable to everyone, formed an exclusive coterie; and as for the rest, they were either old or dull, or both. He often debated whether he should seek out Mr Aked, who was now recovered, and had once, unfortunately in Richard's absence, called at the office; but at length he timidly decided that the extent of their acquaintance would not warrant it.

'Where shall we go to lunch to-day?' was almost the first question which Richard and Jenkins asked each other in the morning, and a prolonged discussion would follow. They called the meal 'lunch,' but it was really their dinner, though neither of them ever admitted the fact.

Jenkins had a predilection for grill-rooms, where raw chops and steaks lay on huge dishes, and each customer chose his own meat and superintended its cooking. A steak, tender and perfectly cooked, with baked potatoes and half a pint of stout, was his ideal repast, and he continually lamented that no restaurant in London offered such cheer at the price of one shilling and threepence, including the waiter. The cheap establishments were never satisfactory, and Jenkins only frequented them when the state of his purse left no alternative. In company with Richard he visited every new eating-house that made its appearance, in the hope of finding the restaurant of his dreams, and though each was a disappointment, yet the search still went on. The place which most nearly coincided with his desires was the 'Sceptre,' a low, sombre room between the Law Courts and the river, used by well-to-do managing clerks and a sprinkling of junior barristers. Here, lounging luxuriously on red plush seats, and in the full sight and hearing of a large silver grill, the two spent many luncheon hours, eating slowly, with gross, sensual enjoyment, and secretly elated by the proximity of men older and more prosperous than themselves, whom they met on equal terms.

Richard once suggested that they should try one of the French restaurants in Soho which Mr Aked had mentioned.

'Not me!' said Jenkins, in reply. 'You don't catch me going to those parley-voo shops again. I went once. They give you a lot of little messes, faked up from yesterday's dirty plates, and after you've eaten half a dozen of 'em you don't feel a bit fuller. Give me a steak and potato. I like to know what I'm eating.'

He had an equal detestation of vegetarian restaurants, but once, during a period of financial depression, he agreed to accompany Richard, who knew the place fairly well, to the 'Crabtree' in Charing Cross Road, and though he grumbled roundly at the insubstantiality of the three-course dinner à la carte which could be obtained for eightpence, he made no difficulty, afterwards, about dining there whenever prudence demanded the narrowest economy.

An air of chill and prim discomfort pervaded the Crabtree, and the mingled odour of lentils and sultana pudding filled every corner. The tables were narrow, and the chairs unyielding. The customers were for the most eccentric as to dress and demeanour; they had pale faces, and during their melancholy meals perused volumes obviously instructive, or debated the topics of the day in platitudinous conversations unspiced by a single oath. Young women with whom their personal appearance was a negligible quantity came in large numbers, and either giggled to one another without restraint or sat erect and glared at the males in a manner which cowed even Jenkins. The waitresses lacked understanding, and seemed to resent even the most courteous advances.

One day, just as they were beginning dinner, Jenkins eagerly drew Richard's attention to the girl at the pay-desk. 'See that girl?' he said.

'What about her? Is she a new one?'

'Why, she's the tart that old Aked used to be after.'

'Was she at that A.B.C. shop in the Strand?' said Richard, who began to remember the girl's features and her reddish brown hair.

'Yes, that's her. Before she was at the A.B.C. she was cashier at the boiled-beef place opposite the Courts, but they say she got the sack for talking to customers too much. She and Aked were very thick then, and he went there every day. I suppose his courting interfered with business.'

'But he's old enough to be her father!'

'Yes. He ought to have been ashamed of himself. She's not a bad kind, eh?'

'There wasn't anything between them, really, was there?'

'*I* don't know. There might have been. He followed her to the A.B.C., and I think he sometimes took her home. Her name's Roberts. We used to have him on about her – rare fun.'

The story annoyed Richard, for his short *tête-à-tête* with Mr Aked had remained in his mind as a pleasant memory, and though he was aware that the old man had been treated with scant respect by the youngsters in the office, he had acquired the habit of mentally regarding him with admiration, as a representative of literature. This attachment to a restaurant cashier, clearly a person of no refinement or intellect, scarcely fitted with his estimate of the journalist who had spoken to Carlyle.

During the meal he surreptitiously glanced at the girl several times. She was plumper than before, and her cough seemed to be cured. Her face was pleasant, and undoubtedly she had a magnificent coiffure.

When they presented their checks, Jenkins bowed awkwardly, and she smiled. He swore to Richard that next time he would mention Mr Aked's name to her. The vow was broken. She was willing to exchange civilities, but her manner indicated with sufficient clearness that a line was to be drawn.

In the following week, when Richard happened to be at the Crabtree alone, at a later hour than usual, they had rather a long conversation.

'Is Mr Aked still at your office?' she asked, looking down at her account books.

Richard told what he knew.

'Oh!' she said, 'I often used to see him, and he gave me some lozenges that cured a bad cough I had. Nice old fellow, wasn't he?'

'Yes, I fancy so,' Richard assented.

'I thought I'd just ask, as I hadn't seen him about for a long time.'

'Good afternoon – Miss Roberts.'

'Good afternoon – Mr ——'

'Larch.'

They both laughed.

A trivial dispute with Jenkins, a few days later, disclosed the fact that that haunter of bars had a sullen temper, and that his displeasure, once aroused, was slow to disappear. Richard dined alone at the Crabtree, and after another little conversation with Miss Roberts, having time at his disposal, he called at the public library in St Martin's Lane. In a half-crown review he saw an article, by a writer of considerable repute, entitled 'To Literary Aspirants,' which purported to demonstrate that a mastery of the craft of words was only to be attained by a regular course of technical exercises; the nature of these exercises was described in detail. There were references to the unremitting drudgery of Flaubert, de Maupassant, and Stevenson, together with extracts chosen to illustrate the slow passage of the last-named author from inspired incompetence to the serene and perfect proficiency before which all difficulties melted. After an unqualified statement that any man – slowly if without talent, quickly if gifted by nature – might with determined application learn to write finely, the essayist concluded by remarking that never before in the history of literature had young authors been so favourably circumstanced as at the present. Lastly came the maxim, *Nulla dies sine linea.*

Richard's cooling enthusiasm for letters leaped into flame. He had done no writing whatever for several weeks, but that night saw him desperately at work. He took advantage of the quarrel to sever all save the most formal connection with Jenkins, dined always frugally at the Crabtree, and spent every evening at his lodging. The thought of Alphonse Daudet writing 'Les Amoureuses' in a Parisian garret supported him through an entire month of toil, during which, besides assiduously practising the recommended exercises, he wrote a complete short story and began several essays. About this time his 'City of Sleep' was returned upon his hands in a condition so filthy and ragged that he was moved to burn it. The short story was offered to an evening daily, and never heard of again.

It occurred to him that possibly he possessed some talent for dramatic criticism, and one Saturday evening he went to the first performance of a play at the St George's theatre. After waiting an hour outside, he got a seat in the last row of the pit. Eagerly he watched the critics take their places in the stalls; they chatted languidly, smiling and bowing now and then to acquaintants in the boxes and dress circle; the pit was excited and loquacious, and Richard discovered that nearly everyone round about him made a practice of attending first nights, and had an intimate knowledge of the *personnel* of the stage. Through the hum of voices the overture to 'Rosamund' fitfully reached him. During whole bars the music was lost; then some salient note caught the ear, and the melody became audible again until another wave of conversation engulfed it.

The conclusion of the last act was greeted with frenzied hand-clapping, beating of sticks, and inarticulate cries, while above the general noise was heard the repeated monosyllable "'thor, 'thor.' After what seemed an interminable delay the curtain was drawn back at one side and a tall man in evening dress, his face a dead white, stepped before the footlights and bowed several times; the noise rose to a thunderous roar, in which howls and hissing were distinguishable. Richard shook from head to foot, and tears unaccountably came to his eyes.

The whole of Sunday and Monday evening were occupied in writing a detailed analysis and appreciation of the play. On Tuesday morning he bought a weekly paper which devoted special attention to the drama, in order to compare his own view with that of an acknowledged authority, and found that the production was dismissed in ten curt lines as mere amiable drivel.

A few days afterwards Mr Curpet offered him the position of cashier in the office, at a salary of three pounds a week. His income was exactly doubled, and the disappointments of unsuccessful authorship suddenly ceased to trouble him. He began to doubt the wisdom of making any further attempt towards literature. Was it not clear that his talents lay in the direction of business? Nevertheless a large part of his spare cash was devoted to the purchase of books, chiefly the productions of a few celebrated old continental presses, which he had recently learned to value. He prepared a scheme for educating himself in the classical tongues and in French, and the practice of writing was abandoned to make opportunity for the pursuit of culture. But culture proved to be shy and elusive. He adhered to no regular course of study, and though he read much, his progress towards knowledge was almost imperceptible.

Other distractions presented themselves in the shape of music and painting. He discovered that he was not without critical taste in both these arts, and he became a frequenter of concerts and picture-galleries. He bought a piano on the hire-purchase system, and took lessons thereon. In this and other ways his expenditure swelled till it more than swallowed up the income of three pounds a week which not long before he had regarded as something very like wealth. For many weeks he made no effort to adjust the balance, until his debts approached the sum of twenty pounds, nearly half of which was owing to his landlady. He had to go through more than one humiliating scene before an era of economy set in.

One afternoon he received a telegram to say that William Vernon had died very suddenly. It was signed 'Alice Clayton Vernon.' Mrs Vernon was William's stately cousin-in-law, and Richard, to whom she had spoken only once, – soon after Mary's wedding, – regarded her with awe; he disliked her because he found it impossible to be at ease in her imposing presence. As he went into Mr Curpet's room to ask for leave of absence, his one feeling was annoyance at the prospect of having to meet her again. William's death, to his own astonishment, scarcely affected him at all.

Mr Curpet readily granted him two days' holiday, and he arranged to go down to Bursley the following night for the funeral.

VIII

Wearied of sitting, Richard folded his overcoat pillow-wise, put it under his head, and extended himself on the polished yellow wood. But in vain were his eyes shut tight. Sleep would not come, though he yawned incessantly. The monstrous beat of the engine, the quick rattle of windows, and the grinding of wheels were fused into a fantastic resonance which occupied every corner of the carriage and invaded his very skull. Then a light tapping on the roof, one of those mysterious sounds which make a compartment in a night-train like a haunted room, momentarily silenced everything else, and he wished that he had not been alone.

Suddenly jumping up, he put away all idea of sleep, and lowered the window. It was pitch dark; vague changing shapes, which might have been either trees or mere fancies of the groping eye, outlined themselves a short distance away; far in front was a dull glare from the engine, and behind twinkled the guard's lamp. . . . In a few seconds he closed the window again, chilled to the bone, though May was nearly at an end.

The thought occurred to him that he was now a solitary upon the face of the earth. It concerned no living person whether he did evil or good. If he chose to seek ruin, to abandon himself to the most ignoble impulses, there was none to restrain, – not even a brother-in-law. For several weeks past, he had been troubled about his future, afraid to face it. Certainly London satisfied him, and the charm of living there had not perceptibly grown less. He rejoiced in London, in its vistas, its shops, its unending crowds, its vastness, its wickedness; each dream dreamed about London in childhood had come true; and surer than ever before was the consciousness that in going to London he had fulfilled his destiny. Yet there was something to lack in himself. His confidence in his own abilities and his own character was being undermined. Nearly a year had gone, and he had made no progress, except at the office. Resolutions were constantly broken; it was three months since he had despatched an article to a newspaper. He had not even followed a definite course of study, and though his acquaintance with modern French fiction had widened, he could boast no exact scholarship even in that piquant field. Evening after evening – ah! those long, lamplit evenings which were to be given to strenuous effort! – was frittered away upon mean banalities, sometimes in the company of some casual acquaintance and sometimes alone. He had by no means grasped the full import and extent of this retrogression; it was merely beginning to disturb his complacence, and perhaps, ever so slightly, his sleep. But now, hurrying to the funeral of William Vernon, he lazily laughed at himself for having allowed his peace of mind to be ruffled. Why bother about 'getting on'? What did it matter?

He still experienced but little sorrow at the death of Vernon. His affection for the man had strangely faded. During the nine months that he had lived in London they had scarcely written to one another, and Richard regarded the long journey to attend William's obsequies as a tiresome concession to propriety.

That was his real attitude, had he cared to examine it.

At about four o'clock it was quite light, and the risen sun woke Richard from a brief doze. The dew lay in the hollows of the fields, but elsewhere there was a soft, fresh clearness which gave to the common incidents of the flying landscape a new and virginal beauty – as though that had been the morn of creation itself. The cattle were stirring, and turned to watch the train as it slipped by.

Richard opened the window again. His mood had changed, and he felt unreasonably joyous. Last night he had been too pessimistic. Life lay yet before him, and time enough to rectify any indiscretions of which he might have been guilty. The future was his, to use as he liked. Magnificent, consoling thought! Moved by some symbolic association of ideas, he put his head out of the window and peered in the direction of the train's motion. A cottage stood alone in the midst of innumerable meadows; as it crossed his vision, the door opened, and a young woman came out with an empty pail swinging in her left hand. Apparently she would be about twenty-seven, plump and sturdy and straight. Her hair was loose about her round, contented face, and with her disengaged hand she rubbed her eyes, still puffed and heavy with sleep. She wore a pink print gown, the bodice of which was unfastened, disclosing a white undergarment and the rich hemispheres of her bosom. In an instant the scene was hidden by a curve of the line, and the interminable succession of fields resumed, but Richard had time to guess from her figure that the woman was the mother of a small family. He pictured her husband still unconscious in the warm bed which she had just left; he even saw the impress of her head on the pillow, and a long nightdress thrown hastily across a chair.

He was deeply and indescribably affected by this suggestion of peaceful married love set in so great a solitude. The woman and her hypothetical husband and children were only peasants, their lives were probably narrow and their intellects dormant, yet they aroused in him a feeling of envy which surged about his brain and for the moment asphyxiated thought. . . .

Later on the train slackened speed as it passed through a shunting-yard. The steam from the light shunting-engine rose with cloud-like delicacy in the clear air, and an occasional short whistle seemed to have something of the quality of a bird's note. The men with their long poles moved blithely among the medley of rails, signalling one another with motions of the arm. The coupling-chains rang with a merry, giant tinkle, and when the engine brought its load of waggons to a standstill, and a smart, metallic bump, bump, bump, ran *diminuendo* from waggon to waggon, one might have fancied that some leviathan game was being played. Richard forgot the girl with the pail, and soon after went to sleep.

At six o'clock the train reached Stoke, where he had to change. Two women with several children also alighted, and he noticed how white and fatigued were their faces; the children yawned pitifully. An icy, searching wind blew through the station; the exhilaration of the dawn was gone, and a spirit of utter woe and disaster brooded over everything. For the first time William's death really touched him.

The streets of Bursley were nearly empty as he walked through the town from the railway station, for the industrial population was already at work in the manufactories, and the shops not yet open. Yet Richard avoided the main thoroughfares, choosing a circuitous route to Shawport lest he might by chance encounter an acquaintance. He foresaw the inevitable banal dialogue:–

'Well, how do you like London?'

'Oh, it's fine!'

'Getting on all right?'

'Yes, thanks.'

And then the effort of two secretly bored persons to continue a perfunctory conversation unaided by a single mutual interest.

A carriage was driving away from the Red House just as Richard got within sight of it; he nodded to the venerable coachman, who gravely touched his hat. The owner of the carriage was Mr Clayton Vernon, William's cousin and an alderman of Bursley, and Richard surmised that Mrs Clayton Vernon had put herself in charge of the place until the funeral should be over. He trembled at the prospect of a whole day to be spent in the company of these excellent people, whom William had always referred to with a smile, and yet not without a great deal of respect. The Clayton Vernons were the chief buttress of respectability in the town; rich, strictly religious, philanthropic, and above all dignified. Everyone looked up to them instinctively, and had they possessed but once vice between them, they would have been loved.

Mrs Clayton Vernon herself opened the door. She was a stately woman of advanced middle age, with a suave, imperious manner.

'I left Clayton to have breakfast by himself,' she said, as she led Richard into the sitting-room; 'I thought you would like someone here to welcome you after your long night journey. Breakfast will be ready almost directly. How tired you must be! Clayton said it was a pity you should come by the night train, but of course it is quite right that you should inconvenience your employers as little as possible, quite right. And we admire you for it. Now will you run upstairs and wash? You've not forgotten the way? . . .'

The details of the funeral had been settled by Mr Clayton Vernon, who was the chief mourner, and Richard had nothing to do but fall in with preconcerted plans and answer decorously when spoken to. The arrangement was satisfactory in that it relieved him from duties which would have been irksome, but scarcely gratifying to his pride. He had lived nearly all his life in that house, and had known the dead man perhaps more intimately than anyone else present. However, he found it convenient to efface himself.

In the evening there was an elaborate tea at which were present the Clayton Vernons and the minister who had conducted the funeral service. The minister and the alderman left immediately afterwards to attend a meeting, and when they were gone Mrs Clayton Vernon said, –

'Now we are all alone, Richard. Go into the drawing-room and I will follow. I do want to have a chat with you.'

She came in with needle and thread and scissors.

'If you will take off your coat, I will stitch on that button that is hanging by one thread, I noticed it this morning, and then it went quite out of my mind. I am so sorry!'

'Oh, thanks!' he blushed hotly. 'But I can stitch myself, you know –'

'Come, you needn't be shy of an old woman seeing you in your shirt-sleeves. Do as I ask.'

He doffed the coat.

'I always like young men to be immaculately neat,' she said, cutting off a piece of cotton. 'One's personal appearance is an index to one's character, don't you think? Of course you do. Here, thread the needle for me. I am afraid since your dear sister died you have grown a little careless, eh? She was *most* particular. Ah, what a mother she was to you!'

'Yes,' said Richard.

'I was very grieved to see you go to the funeral in a soft hat – Richard, really I was. It wasn't respectful to your brother-in-law's memory.'

'I never thought. You see, I started in rather a hurry.' The fact was that he had no silk hat, nor could he easily afford to buy one.

'But you *should* think, my dear boy. Even Clayton was shocked. Are those your best clothes?'

Richard answered that they were. He sheepishly protested that he never bothered about clothes.

There was a silence, broken by her regular stitching. At last she handed him the coat and helped him to put it on. He went to the old green sofa, and somewhat to his dismay she sat down by his side.

'Richard,' she began, in a changed, soft voice, and not without emotion, 'do you know we are expecting great things from you?'

'But you shouldn't. I'm a very ordinary sort of person.'

'No, no. That you are not! God has given you great talents, and you must use them. Poor William always used to say that you were highly gifted and might do great things.'

'Might!'

'Yes – if you tried.'

'But, how am I gifted? And what "great things" are expected?' he asked, perhaps angling for further flattering disclosures.

'I cannot answer that,' said Mrs Clayton Vernon; 'it is for you to answer. You have given all your friends the impression that you would do something worth doing. You have raised hopes, and you must not disappoint them. We believe in you, Richard. That is all I can say.'

'That's all very well; but——' He stopped and played with the seal on his watch-chain. 'The fact is, I am working, you know. I want to be an author – at least a journalist.'

'Ah!'

'It's a slow business – at first –' Suddenly moved to be confidential, he went on to give her some account, incomplete and judiciously edited, of his life during the past year.

'You have relieved my mind greatly, and Clayton will be so glad. We were beginning to think——'

'Why were you "beginning to think"?'

'Well, never mind now.'

'But why?'

'Never mind. I have full confidence in you, and I am sure you will get on. Poor boy, you have no near connections or relatives now?'

'No, none.'

'You must look on Clayton and myself as very near relatives. We have no children, but our hearts are large. I shall expect you to write to me sometimes and to come and stay with us now and then.'

IX

In the centre of the reading-room at the British Museum sit four men fenced about by a quadruple ring of unwieldy volumes which are an index to all the knowledge in the world. The four men know those volumes as a good courier knows the Continental Bradshaw, and all day long, from early morning, when the attendants, self-propelled on wheeled stools, run round the rings arranging and aligning the huge blue tomes, to late afternoon, when the immense dome is like a dark night and the arc lamps hiss and crackle in the silence, they answer questions, patiently, courteously; they are seldom embarrassed and less seldom in the wrong.

Radiating in long rows from the central fortress of learning a diversified company of readers disposes itself: bishops, statesmen, men of science, historians, needy pedants, popular authors whose broughams are waiting in the precincts, journalists, medical students, law students, curates, hack-writers, women with clipped hair and black aprons, idlers; all short-sighted and all silent.

Every few minutes an official enters in charge of an awed group of country visitors, and whispers mechanically the unchanging formula: 'Eighty thousand volumes in this room alone: thirty-six miles of bookshelves in the Museum altogether.' Whereupon the visitors stare about them, the official unsuccessfully endeavours not to let it appear that the credit of the business belongs entirely to himself, and the party retires again.

Vague, reverberating noises roll heavily from time to time across the chamber, but no one looks up; the incessant cannibal feast of the living upon the dead goes speechlessly forward; the trucks of food are always moving to and fro, and the nonchalant waiters seem to take no rest.

Almost Richard's first care on coming to London had been to obtain a reader's ticket for the British Museum, and for several months he had made a practice of spending Saturday afternoon there, following no special line of study or research, and chiefly contenting himself with desultory reading in the twenty thousand volumes which could be reached down without the slow machinery of an order form. After a time the charm of the place had dwindled, and other occupations filled his Saturday afternoons.

But when upon his return from William's funeral he stepped from Euston Station into Bloomsbury, the old enthusiasms came back in all their original freshness. The seduction of the street vistas, the lofty buildings, and the swiftly flitting hansoms once more made mere wayfaring a delight; the old feeling of self-confident power lifted his chin, and the failures of the past were forgotten in a dream of future possibilities. He dwelt with pleasure on that part of his conversation with Mrs Clayton Vernon which disclosed the interesting fact that Bursley would be hurt if he failed to do 'things'. Bursley, and especially Mrs Clayton Vernon, good woman, should not be disappointed. He had towards his native town the sentiments of a consciously clever husband who divines an admiring trust in the glance of a little ignoramus of a wife. Such faith was indeed touching.

One of the numerous resolutions which he made was to resume attendance at the British Museum; the first visit was anticipated with impatience, and when he found himself once more within the book-lined walls of the reading-room he was annoyed to discover that his plans for study were not matured sufficiently to enable him to realise any definite part of them, however small, that day. An idea for an article on 'White Elephants' was nebulous in his brain; he felt sure that the subject might be treated in a fascinating manner, if only he could put his hands on the right material. An hour passed in searching Poole's Index and other works of reference, without result, and Richard spent the remainder of the afternoon in evolving from old magazines schemes for articles which would present fewer difficulties in working out. Nothing of value was accomplished, and yet he experienced neither disappointment nor a sense of failure. Contact with innumerable books of respectable but forbidding appearance had cajoled him, as frequently before, into the delusion that he had been industrious; surely it was impossible that a man could remain long in that atmosphere of scholarly attainment without acquiring knowledge and improving his mind!

Presently he abandoned the concoction of attractive titles for his articles, and began to look through some volumes of the 'Biographie Universelle.' The room was thinning now. He glanced at the clock; it was turned six. He had been there nearly four hours! With a sigh of satisfaction he replaced all his books and turned to go, mentally discussing whether or not so much application did not entitle him, in spite of certain resolutions, to go to the Ottoman that evening.

'Hey!' a voice called out as he passed the glass screen near the door; it sang resonantly among the desks and ascended into the dome; a number of readers looked up. Richard turned round sharply, and beheld Mr Aked moving a forefinger on the other side of the screen.

'Been here long?' the older man asked, when Richard had come round to him. 'I've been here all day, – first time for fifteen years at least. Strange we didn't see each other. They've got a beastly new regulation about novels less than five years old not being available. I particularly wanted some of Gissing's – not for the mere fun of reading 'em of course, because I've read 'em before. I wanted them for a special purpose – I may tell you about it some day – and I couldn't get them, at least several of them. What a tremendous crowd there is here nowadays!'

'Well, you see, it's Saturday afternoon,' Richard put in, 'and Saturday afternoon's the only time that most people can come, unless they're men of independent means like yourself. You seem to have got a few novels besides Gissing's though.' About forty volumes were stacked upon Mr Aked's desk, many of them open.

'Yes, but I've done now.' He began to close the books with a smack and to pitch them down roughly in new heaps, exactly like a petulant boy handling school-books. 'See, pile them between my arms, and I bet you I'll carry them away all at once.'

'Oh, no. I'll help you,' Richard laughed. 'It'll be far less trouble than picking up what you drop.'

While they were waiting at the centre desk Mr Aked said, –

'There's something about this place that makes you ask for more volumes than can possibly be useful to you. I question whether I've done any good here to-day at all. If I'd been content with three or four books instead of thirty or forty, I might have done something. By the way, what are you here for?'

'Well, I just came to look up a few points,' Richard answered vaguely. 'I've been messing about – got a notion or two for articles, that's all.'

Mr Aked stopped to shake hands as soon as they were outside the Museum. Richard was very disappointed that their meeting should have been so short. This man of strange vivacity had thrown a spell over him. Richard was sure that his conversation, if only he could be persuaded to talk, would prove delightfully original and suggestive; he guessed that they were mutually sympathetic. Ever since their encounter in the A.B.C. shop Richard had desired to know more of him, and now, when by chance they had met again, Mr Aked's manner showed little or no inclination towards a closer acquaintance. There was of course a difference between them in age of at least thirty years, but to Richard that seemed no bar to an intimacy. It was, he surmised, only the physical part of Mr Aked that had grown old.

'Well, good-bye.'

'Good-bye.' Should he ask if he might call at Mr Aked's rooms or house, or whatever his abode was? He hesitated, from nervousness.

'Often come here?'

'Generally on Saturdays,' said Richard.

'We may see each other again, then, sometime. Good-bye.'

Richard left him rather sadly, and the sound of the old man's quick, alert footsteps – he almost stamped – receded in the direction of Southampton Row. A minute later, as Richard was turning round by Mudie's out of Museum Street, a hand touched his shoulder. It was Mr Aked's.

'By the way,' the man's face crinkled into a smile as he spoke, 'are you doing anything to-night?'

'Nothing whatever.'

'Let's go and have dinner together – I know a good French place in Soho.'

'Oh, thanks. I shall be awfully pleased.'

'Half a crown, *table d'hôte*. Can you afford?'

'Certainly I can,' said Richard, perhaps a little annoyed, until he recollected that Mr Aked had used exactly the same phrase on a previous occasion.

'I'll pay for the wine.'

'Not at all –'

'I'll pay for the wine,' Mr Aked repeated decisively.

'All right. You told me about this Soho place before, if you remember.'

'So I did, so I did, so I did.'

'What made you turn back?'

'A whim, young friend, nothing else. Take my arm.'

Richard laughed aloud, for no reason in particular except that he felt happy. They settled to a brisk walk.

The restaurant was a square apartment with a low and smoky beamed ceiling, and shining brass hat-pegs all round the walls; above the hat-pegs were framed advertisements of liqueurs and French, Italian, and Spanish wines. The little tables, whose stiff snowy cloths came near to touching the floor at every side, gleamed and glittered in the light of a fire. The place was empty save for an old waiter who was lighting the gas. The waiter turned a large, mild countenance to Mr Aked as the two entered, and smiling benignly greeted him with a flow of French, and received a brief reply in the same language. Richard failed to comprehend what was said.

They chose a table near the fire. Mr Aked at once pulled a book from his pocket and began to read; and Richard, somewhat accustomed by this time to his peculiarities, found nothing extraordinary in such conduct. This plain little restaurant seemed full of enchantment. He was in Paris, – not the great Paris which is reached *via* Charing Cross, but that little Paris which hides itself in the immensity of London. French newspapers were scattered about the room; the sound of French voices came musically through an open door; the bread which was presently brought in with the *hors d'œuvres* was French, and the setting of the table itself showed an exotic daintiness which he had never seen before.

Outside a barrel organ was piercingly strident in the misty dusk. Above the ground-glass panes of the window, Richard could faintly descry the upper storeys of houses on the opposite side of the road. There was a black and yellow sign, 'Umberto Club,' and above that a blue and red sign, 'Blanchisserie française.' Still higher was an open window from which leaned a young, negligently dressed woman with a coarse Southern face; she swung a bird-cage idly in her hand; the bird-cage fell and was swallowed by the ground glass, and the woman with a gesture of despair disappeared from the window; the barrel organ momentarily ceased its melody and then struck up anew.

Everything seemed strangely, delightfully unsubstantial, even the meek, bland face of the waiter as he deftly poured out the soup. Mr Aked, having asked for the wine list, called 'Cinquante, Georges, s'il vous plait,' and divided his attention impartially between the soup and his book. Richard picked up the 'Echo de Paris' which lay on a neighbouring chair. On the first page was a reference in displayed type to the success of the fueilleton '*de notre collaborateur distingué*, Catulle Mendès. How wondrously enticing the feuilleton looked, with its descriptive paragraphs cleverly diversified by short lines of dialogue, and at the end 'CATULLE MENDÈS, *à suivre. Reproduction interdite!*' Half Paris, probably, was reading that feuilleton! Catulle Mendès was a real man, and no doubt eating his dinner at that moment!

When the fish came, and Georges had gently poured out the wine, Mr Aked's tongue was loosed.

'And how has the Muse been behaving herself?' he began.

Richard told him, with as little circumlocution as pride would allow, the history of the last few sterile months.

'I suppose you feel a bit downhearted.'

'Not in the least!' answered Richard, bravely, and just then his reply was approximately true.

'*Never* feel downhearted?'

'Well, of course one gets a bit sick sometimes.'

'Let's see, to-day's the 30th. How many words have you written this month?'

'How many words!' Richard laughed. 'I never count what I do in that way. But it's not much. I haven't felt in the humour. There was the funeral. That put me off.'

'I suppose you think you must write only *when the mood is on you.*' Mr Aked spoke sarcastically, and then laughed. 'Quite a mistake. I'll give you this bit of advice and charge nothing for it. Sit down every night and write five hundred words descriptive of some scene which has occurred during the day. Never mind how tired you are; do it. Do it for six months, and then compare the earlier work with the later, and you'll keep on.'

Richard drank the wisdom in.

'Did you do that once?'

'I did, sir. Everyone does it that comes to anything. I didn't come to anything, though I made a bit of money at one time. But then mine was a queer case. I was knocked over by dyspepsia. Beware of dyspepsia. I was violently dyspeptic for twenty years – simply couldn't write. Then I cured myself. But it was too late to begin again.' He spoke in gulps between mouthfuls of fish.

'How did you cure yourself?'

The man took no notice of the question, and went on:–

'And if I haven't written anything for twenty years, I'm still an author at heart. In fact, I've got something 'in the air' now. Oh! I've always had the literary temperament badly. Do you ever catch yourself watching instinctively for the characteristic phrase?'

'I'm afraid I don't quite know what you mean.'

'Eh?'

Richard repeated what he had said, but Mr Aked was absorbed in pouring out another glass of wine.

'I wish you'd tell me,' Richard began, after a pause, 'how you first *began* to write, or rather to get printed.'

'My dear little friend, I can't tell you anything new. I wrote for several years and never sold a line. And for what peculiar reason, should you think? Simply because not a line was worth printing. Then my things began to be accepted. I sold a story first; I forget the title, but I remember there was a railway accident in it, and it happened to come before the editor of a magazine just when everyone was greatly excited about a railway smash in the West of England. I got thirty shillings for that.'

'I think I should get on all right enough if only I could sell *one* thing.' Richard sighed.

'Well, you must wait. Why, damn it all, man!' – he stopped to drink, and Richard noticed how his hand shook. 'How long have you been working seriously? Not a year! If you were going in for painting, you surely wouldn't expect to sell pictures after only a year's study?' Mr Aked showed a naïve appreciation of himself in the part of a veteran who deigns to give a raw recruit the benefit of vast experience.

'Of course not,' assented Richard, abashed.

'Well, then, don't begin to whine.'

After the cheese Mr Aked ordered coffee and cognac, and sixpenny cigars. They smoked in silence.

'Do you know,' Richard blurted out at length, 'the fact is I'm not sure that I'm meant for writing at all. I never take any pleasure *in* writing. It's a confounded nuisance.' He almost trembled with apprehension as he uttered the words.

'You like thinking about what you're going to write, arranging, observing, etc.?'

'Yes, I like that awfully.'

'Well, here's a secret. No writer does like writing, at least not one in a hundred, and the exception, ten to one, is a howling mediocrity. That's a fact. But all the same they're miserable if they don't write.'

'I'm glad; there's hope.'

When Richard had finished his coffee, it occurred to him to mention Miss Roberts.

'Do you ever go to the Crabtree?' he asked.

'Not of late.'

'I only ask because there's a girl there who knows you. She inquired of me how you were not long since.'

'A girl who knows me? Who the devil may she be?'

'I fancy her name's Roberts.'

'Aha! So she's got a new place, has she? She lives in my street. That's how I know her. Nice little thing, rather!'

He made no further remark on the subject, but there remained an absent, amused smile on his face, and he pulled at his lower lip and fastened his gaze on the table.

'You must come down sometime, and see me; my niece keeps house for me,' he said before they separated, giving an address in Fulham. He wrung Richard's hand, patted him on the shoulder, winking boyishly, and went off whistling to himself very quietly in the upper register.

X

The slender, badly hung gate closed of itself behind him with a resounding clang, communicating a little thrill to the ground.

In answer to his ring a girl came to the door. She was rather short, thin, and dressed in black, with a clean white apron. In the half light of the narrow lobby he made out a mahogany hat-rack of conventional shape, and on a wooden bracket a small lamp with a tarnished reflector.

'No,' Richard heard in a quiet, tranquil voice, 'Mr Aked has just gone out for a walk. He didn't say what time he should be back. Can I give him any message?'

'He sent me a card to come down and see him this afternoon, and –

I've come. He said about seven o'clock. It's a quarter past now. But perhaps he forgot all about it.'

'Will you step inside? He may only be away for a minute or two.'

'No, thanks. If you'll just tell him I've called –'

'I'm so sorry –' The girl raised her hand and rested it against the jamb of the doorway; her eyes were set slantwise on the strip of garden, and she seemed to muse an instant.

'Are you Mr Larch?' she asked hesitatingly, just as Richard was saying good-day.

'Yes,' answered Richard.

'Uncle was telling me he had had dinner with you. I'm *sure* he'll be back soon. Won't you wait a little while?'

'Well –'

She stood aside, and Richard passed into the lobby.

The front room, into which he was ushered, was full of dim shadows, attributable to the multiplicity of curtains which obscured the small bay window. Carteret Street and the half-dozen florid, tawny, tree-lined avenues that run parallel to it contain hundreds of living rooms almost precisely similar. Its dimensions were thirteen feet by eleven, and the height of the ceiling appeared to bring the walls, which were papered in an undecipherable pattern of blue, even closer together than they really were. Linoleum with a few rugs served for a carpet. The fireplace was of painted stone, and a fancy screen of South African grasses hid the grate. Behind a clock and some vases on the mantelpiece rose a confection of walnut and silvered glass. A mahogany chiffonier filled the side of the room farthest from the window; it had a marble top and a large mirror framed in scroll work, and was littered with salt-cellars, fruit plates, and silver nicknacks. The table, a square one, was covered by a red cloth of flannel-like texture patterned in black. The chairs were of mahogany and horsehair, and matched the sofa, which stretched from the door nearly to the window. Several prints framed in gilt and oak depended by means of stout green cord from French nails with great earthenware heads. In the recess to the left of the hearth stood a piano, open, and a song on the music-stand. What distinguished the room from others of its type was a dwarf bookcase filled chiefly with French novels whose vivid yellow gratefully lightened a dark corner next the door.

'Uncle is very forgetful,' the girl began. There was some sewing on the table, and she had already taken it up. Richard felt shy and ill at ease, but his companion showed no symptom of discomposure. He smiled vaguely, not knowing what to reply.

'I suppose he walks a good deal,' he said at length.

'Yes, he does.' There was a second pause. The girl continued to sew quietly; she appeared to be indifferent whether they conversed or not.

'I see you are a musician.'

'Oh, no!' she laughed, and looked at his eyes. 'I sing a very little bit.'

'Do you sing Schubert's songs?'

'Schubert's? No. Are they good?'

'Rather. They're *the* songs.'

'Classical, I suppose.' Her tone implied that classical songs were outside the region of the practical.

'Yes, of course.'

'I don't think I care much for classical music.'

'But you should.'

'Should I? Why?' She laughed gaily, like a child amused. 'Hope Temple's songs are nice, and 'The River of Years,' I'm just learning that. Do you sing?'

'No – I don't really sing. I haven't got a piano at my place – now.'

'What a pity! I suppose you know a great deal about music?'

'I wish I did!' said Richard, trying awkwardly not to seem flattered.

A third pause.

'Mr Aked seems to have a fine lot of French novels. I wish I had as many.'

'Yes. He's always bringing them in.'

'And this is the latest, eh?' He picked up 'L'Abbé Tigrane,' which lay on the table by the sewing.

'Yes, I fancy uncle got that last night.'

'You read French, of course?'

'I! No, indeed!' Again she laughed. 'You musn't imagine, Mr Larch,' she went on, and her small eyes twinkled, 'that I am at all like uncle. I'm not. I've only kept house for him a little while, and we are really – quite different.'

'How do you mean, "like uncle"?'

'Well,' the quiet voice was imperceptibly raised, 'I'm not a great reader, and I know nothing of books. I'm not clever, you know. I can't bear poetry.'

Richard looked indulgent.

'But you do read?'

'Yes, sometimes a novel. I'm reading "East Lynne." Uncle bought it for me the other day.'

'And you like it?'

There was a timid tap at the door, and a short, stout servant with red hands and a red face entered; her rough, chubby forearms were bare, and she carried a market basket. 'Please, 'm,' she ejaculated meaningly and disappeared. Mr Aked's niece excused herself, and when she returned Richard looked at his watch and rose.

'I'm very sorry about uncle – but it's just like him.'

'Yes, isn't it?' Richard answered, and they exchanged a smile.

He walked down Carteret Street humming a tuneless air and twirling his stick. Mr Aked's niece had proved rather disappointing. She was an ordinary girl, and evidently quite unsusceptible to the artistic influences which subtly emanated from Mr Aked. But with the exception of his landlady and his landlady's daughter, she was the first woman whom Richard had met in London, and the interview had been somewhat of an ordeal.

Yes, it was matter for regret. Suppose she had been clever, witty, full of that 'nameless charm' with which youths invest the ideal maidens of their dreams – with which, indeed, during the past week he had invested her! He might have married her. Then, guided by the experience of a sympathetic uncle-in-law, he would have realised all his ambitions. A vision of Mr Richard Larch, the well-known editor, and his charming wife, giving a dinner-party to a carefully selected company of literary celebrities, flitted before him. Alas! The girl's 'East Lynne,' her drawing-room ballads, the mean little serving-maid, the complacent vulgarity of the room, the house, the street, the neighbourhood, combined effectually to dispel it.

He felt sure that she had no aspirations.

It was necessary to wait for a train at Parson's Green station. From the elevated platform fields were visible through a gently falling mist. The curving rails stole away mysteriously into a general greyness, and the twilight, assuaging every crudity of the suburban landscape, gave an impression of vast spaces and perfect serenity. Save for the porter leisurely lighting the station lamps, he was alone, – alone, as it seemed to him, in an upper world, above London, and especially above Fulham and the house where lived the girl who read 'East Lynne.' How commonplace must she be! Richard wondered that Mr Aked could exist surrounded by all the banalities of Carteret Street. Even his own lodging was more attractive, for at least Raphael Street was within sound of the central hum and beat of the city.

A signal suddenly shone out in the distance; it might have been a lighthouse seen across unnumbered miles of calm ocean. Rain began to fall.

XI

Richard's Sabbaths had become days of dismal torpor. A year ago, on first arriving in London, he had projected a series of visits to churches famous either for architectural beauty or for picturesque ritual. A few weeks, however, had brought tedium. He was fundamentally irreligious, and his churchgoing proceeded from a craving, purely sensuous, which sought gratification in ceremonial pomps, twilight atmospheres heavy with incense and electric with devotion, and dim perspectives of arching stone. But these things he soon discovered lost their fine savour by the mere presence of a prim congregation secure in the brass armour of self-complacency; for him the worship was spoilt by the worshippers, and so the time came when the only church which he cared to attend – and even to this he went but infrequently, lest use should stale its charm – was the Roman Catholic oratory of St Philip Neri, where the separation of the sexes struck a grateful note of austerity, and the mean appearance of the people contrasted admirably with the splendour of the priests' vestments, the elaborate music, and the gilt and colour of altars. Here deity was omnipotent and humanity abject. Men and women of all grades, casting themselves down before the holy images in the ecstatic abandonment of repentance, prayed side by side, oblivious of everything save their sins and the anger of a God. As a spectacle the service at the oratory was sublime.

He witnessed it about once a month. The mornings of intervening Sundays were given to aimless perambulation of the parks, desultory reading, or sleep; there was nothing to prevent him leaving town for the day, but he was so innocent of any sort of rural lore that the prospect of a few hours in the country was seldom enticing enough to rouse sufficient energy for its accomplishment. After dinner he usually slept, and in the evening he would take a short walk and go early to bed. For some reason he never attempted to work on Sundays.

It had rained continuously since he left Parson's Green station on the previous night, till midday on Sunday, and in the afternoon he was lounging half asleep with a volume of verse on his knee, considering whether or not to put on his hat and go out, when Lily entered; Lily was attired for conquest, and with her broad velvet hat and pink bows looked so unlike a servant-girl that drowsy Richard started up, uncertain what fairy was brightening his room.

'Please, sir, there's a young gentleman as wants to see you.'

'Oh! – who is it?' No one had ever called upon him before.

'I don't know, sir; it's a young *gentleman*.'

The young gentleman was ushered in. He wore a new black frock coat, and light grey trousers which fell in folds over new patent-leather boots. The shortcomings of his linen, which was dull and bluish in tint, were more than atoned for by the magnificence of a new white silk necktie with heliotrope spots. He carried a silk hat and a pair of unworn kid gloves in one hand, and in the other a half-smoked cigar and a stick, with whose physiognomy Richard was quite familiar.

'Hello, Jenkins!'

'Good afternoon, Mr Larch. I was just passing this way, and I thought I'd look you up.' With an inclination of the head more ridiculous even than he intended, Jenkins placed his hat, stick, and gloves on the bed, and, nicely adjusting the tails of his coat, occupied a chair.

The quarrel between Richard and Jenkins had been patched up a few days before.

'So this is your digs. Nice large windows!'

'Yes, decent windows.'

Although these two were on terms of almost brutal familiarity during office hours, here each felt slightly uncomfortable in the other's presence. Jenkins wiped his pallid, unhealthy face with a cambric handkerchief which he unfolded for the purpose.

'Been to church this morning?'

Meditatively Jenkins flicked some cigar-ash into the fire-grate, and then answered, 'Yes.'

'I thought so.'

'Why?'

'Because you're such a swell.'

'Ain't I just!' Jenkins spoke with frank delight. 'Two guineas the suit, my boy! Won't I knock 'em in the Wal–worth Road!'

'But where's your ring?' Richard asked, noticing the absence of the silver ring which Jenkins commonly wore on his left hand.

'Oh! I gave it to my sister. She wanted to give it to her young man.'

'She's engaged, is she?'

'Yes – at least I suppose she is.'

'And when are you going to get engaged?'

Jenkins emitted a sound expressive of scorn. 'You don't catch me entering the holy bonds. Not this child! It ain't all lavender, you bet. I say, you know Miss Roberts at the veg – red-haired tart.' Jenkins was unaware that Richard had been going regularly to the Crabtree. 'I was passing the place last night just as they were closing, and I walked down to Charing Cross with her. I asked her to meet me to-day somewhere, but she couldn't.'

'You mean she wouldn't. Well, and what sort's she?'

'Devilish nice, *I* tell you. But not my style. But there's a girl I know – lives down the Camberwell New Road. She is a treat now, – a fair treat. About seventeen, and plump as a pigeon. I shall see her to-night.'

'Oh, indeed!' said Richard, for the hundredth time marvelling that he should be on a footing of intimacy with Albert Jenkins. The girl at Carteret Street, whatever her imperfections, did not use the Cockney dialect. And her smile was certainly alluring. Moreover, she had dignity. True, she liked 'East Lynne' and Hope Temple's songs, but it occurred to

Richard that it might be pleasanter to listen even to these despised melodies than to remain solitary at Raphael Street or to accompany Jenkins on a *prowl*. Why should he not go down that afternoon to see Mr Aked – and his niece? He immediately decided that he would do so.

'It's turned out fine,' said Jenkins. 'What are you up to to-night? Will you come and have a turn round with me?'

'Let me see . . . The fact is, I can't.' He fought desperately against the temptation to mention that he proposed to call on a lady, but in vain. Forth it must come. 'I'm going to see a girl.'

'Aha!' exclaimed Jenkins, with a terribly arch look. 'So that's the little game, eh! Who's the mash?'

Richard smiled reticently.

'Well, I'll be off.' Jenkins rose, and his eye caught Richard's little bookcase; he scanned the titles of the volumes.

'Oh! Likewise ah! Zola! Now we're getting at the secret. No wonder you're so damn studious. Zola, indeed! Well, so long. See you to-morrow. Give my love to the girl. . . . I say, I suppose you haven't got Zola in English, have you?'

'No.'

'Never mind. So long.'

XII

The little red-armed servant beamed an amiable recognition.

'Very hot day!' Richard said.

'Beg pardon, sir.'

'Very hot day,' rather louder. They were in the passage.

The door of the sitting-room opened, and Mr Aked's niece stood before him, her finger on her lips and her eyebrows raised in a gesture of warning. She suddenly smiled, almost laughed. Richard remembered that smile for a long time afterwards. It transformed not only a girl's face, but the whole of Carteret Street. He had never seen anything like it. Shaking hands in silence, he followed her into the room, and she gently closed the door.

'Uncle's not well,' she explained. 'He's asleep now, and I didn't want you to wake him. In this house, you know, if any one speaks in the passage, you can hear it even in the attic. Uncle was caught in the rain last night; he has a very weak chest, and gets bronchitis directly.'

'I'm awfully sorry I disturbed you,' said Richard. 'The fact is I was down this way, and I thought I'd call.' It sounded a sufficiently reasonable excuse, he considered. 'I hope you weren't asleep too.'

'Yes, I was dozing in this chair.' She put her head back, and drummed her fingers lightly on the arms of the chair. 'But I'm glad you've called.'

'Why?'

'Oh! Because one wants to see some one – some one new, especially after being in a sick-room.'

'You've been sitting up late.' His tone was accusing. It seemed to him that somehow they were already intimate.

'Only till three o'clock, and I slept later this morning. How changeable the sun is to-day!' She moved her chair, and he saw her in profile. Her hands were on her lap. She coaxed a foot-stool into position with her toes, and placed her feet on it.

'You look just like a picture in this week's "Illustrated London News" – I mean in general pose,' he exclaimed.

'Do I? How nice that sounds! What is it?'

'Whistler's "Portrait of his Mother." But I hope you don't think I think you look old.'

'How old do I look?' She turned her head slightly towards him.

'About twenty-three, only I imagine you're much younger.'

Although she did not reply, she made no pretence of being annoyed, nor did Richard tax himself with a *gaucherie*.

'It took me years to like Whistler's pictures,' she said; and in response to Richard's surprised question she was beginning to explain that a large part of her life had been passed in the companionship of works of graphic art, when a slippered step was heard in the hall and some one fumbled with the door-handle. Mr Aked entered.

'Uncle! You wicked old man!' She sprang up, flushed, and her eyes sparkled angrily. 'Whatever did you get up for? It's enough to kill you.'

'Calm yourself, my child. I got up because I didn't want to stay in bed, – exactly that.'

Mr Aked paused to take breath and sank into a chair. 'Larch, I heard your voice in the passage. Upon my word, I quite forgot you yesterday. I suppose Adeline's been telling you I'm seriously ill, eh? Ah! I've had many a worse attack than this. Put that antimacassar over my shoulders, child.'

He had given Richard a hot, limp hand, on which the veins formed soft ridges in the smooth, brittle skin. His grey hair was disarranged, and he wore a dirty, torn dressing-gown. His face had lost its customary alert expression; but his sunk, shining eyes glanced with mysterious restlessness first at Richard, then at Adeline, who, uttering no further word, covered him well and put the hassock under his feet.

'Well, well, well!' he sighed and closed his eyes wearily. The other two sat silent for a time; then Adeline, talking very quietly, and with a composure not quite unaffected, took up their interrupted conversation.

Richard gathered that her justifiable vexation would remain in abeyance till he had gone. Soon her tone grew more natural; she leaned forward with hands clasped round one knee, and Richard felt like a receiver of confidences as she roughly outlined her life in the country which had come to an end only two years ago. Were all girls so simply communicative, he wondered; it pleased him to decide that they were not, and that to any other but himself she would have been more reserved; that there was, in fact, an affinity between them. But the presence of her uncle, which Adeline seemed able to ignore utterly, hindered Richard from being himself.

'How do you like London, after living so long in the country?' he asked inevitably.

'I know practically nothing of London, real London,' she said; 'but I think these suburbs are horrid, – far duller than the dullest village. And the people! They seem so uninteresting, to have no character!'

The hoarse, fatigued voice of Mr Aked crept in between them. 'Child!' he said – and he used the appellation, not with the proper dignity of age, but rather like an omniscient schoolboy, home for the holiday, addressing a sister – 'Child!' – his eyes were still closed, – 'the suburbs, even Walham Green and Fulham, are full of interest, for those who can see it. Walk along this very street on such a Sunday afternoon as to day. The roofs form two horrible, converging straight lines I know, but beneath there is character, individuality, enough to make the greatest book ever written. Note the varying indications supplied by bad furniture seen through curtained windows, like ours' (he grinned, opened his eyes, and sat up) 'listen to the melodies issuing lamely from ill-tuned pianos; examine the enervated figures of women reclining amidst flower-pots on narrow balconies. Even in the thin smoke ascending unwillingly from invisible chimney-pots, the flutter of a blind, the bang of a door, the winking of a fox terrier perched on a window-sill, the colour of paint, the lettering of a name, – in all these things there is character and matter of interest, – truth waiting to be expounded. How many houses are there in Carteret Street? Say eighty. Eighty theatres of love, hate, greed, tyranny, endeavour; eighty separate dramas always unfolding, intertwining, ending, beginning, – and every drama a tragedy. No comedies, and especially no farces! Why, child, there is more character within a hundred yards of this chair than a hundred Balzacs could analyse in a hundred years.'

All the old vivacity had returned to his face; he had been rhetorical on a favourite subject, and he was frankly pleased with himself.

'You will tire yourself, uncle,' said Adeline. 'Shall we have tea?'

Richard observed with astonishment that she was cold and unmoved. Surely she could not be blind to the fact that Mr Aked was a very remarkable man with very remarkable ideas! Why, by the way, had those ideas never presented themselves to *him*? He would write an article on the *character* of Raphael Street. Unwillingly he announced he must go; to remain longer would be to invite himself to tea.

'Sit still, Larch. You'll have a cup of tea.'

Adeline left the room; and when she had gone, Mr Aked, throwing a glance after her, said, –

'Well, what do you think of my notions of the suburb?'

'They are splendid,' Richard replied, glowing.

'There's something in them, I imagine,' he agreed complacently. 'I've had an idea lately of beginning to scribble again. I know there's a book waiting to be written on 'The Psychology of the Suburbs,' and I don't like to see copy lying about wasted. The old war-horse scenting the battle, you understand.' He smiled grandiosely. '"Psychology of the Suburbs"! Fine title that! See how the silent *P* takes away all the crudity of the alliteration; that's because one never listens to words with the ears alone, but with the eyes also. . . . But I should need help. I want a clever chap who can take down from dictation, and assist me in the details of composition. I suppose you wouldn't care to come here two or three evenings a week?'

Richard answered sincerely that nothing would suit him better.

'I should make you joint author, of course "Psychology of the Suburbs," by Richard Aked and Richard Larch. It sounds rather catchy, and I think it ought to sell. About four hundred octavo pages, say a hundred and fifty thousand words. Six shillings – must be popular in price. We might get a royalty of ninepence a copy if we went to the right publisher. Sixpence for me and threepence for you. Would that do?'

'Oh, perfectly!' But was not Mr Aked running on rather fast?

'Perhaps we'd better say fivepence halfpenny for me and threepence halfpenny for you; that would be fairer. Because you'll have to furnish ideas, you know. "Psychology of the Suburbs, Psychology of the Suburbs"! Fine title! We ought to do it in six months.'

'I hope you'll be quite well again soon. Then we——'

'Quite well!' he repeated sharply. 'I shall be as right as a trivet to-morrow. You don't suppose that I can't take care of myself! We'll start at once.'

'You're not forgetting, Mr Aked, that you've never seen any of my stuff yet? Are you sure I shall be able to do what you want?'

'Oh, you'll do. I've not seen your stuff, but I guess you've got the literary habit. The literary habit, that's the thing! I'll soon put you up to the wrinkles, the trade secrets.'

'What is your general plan of the book?' Richard asked with some timidity, fearing to be deemed either stupid or inquisitive at the wrong moment. He had tried to say something meet for a great occasion, and failed.

'Oh! I'll go into that at our first formal conference, say next Friday night. Speaking roughly, each of the great suburban divisions has, for me at any rate, its own characteristics, its peculiar moral physiognomy.' Richard nodded appreciatively. 'Take me blindfold to any street in London, and I'll discover instantly, from a thousand hints, where I am. Well, each of these divisions must be described in turn, not topographically of course, but the inner spirit, the soul of it. See? People have got into a way of sneering at the suburbs. Why, the suburbs *are* London! It is alone the – the concussion of meeting suburbs in the centre of London that makes the city and West End interesting. We could show how the special characteristics of the different suburbs exert a subtle influence on the great central spots. Take Fulham; no one thinks anything of Fulham, but suppose it were swept off the face of the earth the effect would be to alter, for the seeing eye, the character of Piccadilly and the Strand and Cheapside. The play of one suburb on another and on the central haunts is as regular, as orderly, as calculable, as the law of gravity itself.'

They continued the discussion until Adeline came in again with a tray in her hands, followed by the little red-armed servant. The two began to lay the cloth, and the cheerful rattle of crockery filled the room. . . .

'Sugar, Mr Larch?' Adeline was saying, when Mr Aked, looking meaningly at Richard, ejaculated, –

'Friday then?'

Richard nodded. Adeline eyed her uncle distrustfully.

For some reason, unguessed by Richard, Adeline left them alone during most of the evening, and in her absence Mr Aked continued to discourse, in vague generalities not without a special poetical charm, on the subject upon which they were to collaborate, until Richard was wholly intoxicated with its fascinating possibilities. When he left, Adeline would not allow Mr Aked to go to the door, and went herself.

'If I hadn't been very firm,' she laughed as they were shaking hands in the passage, 'uncle would have stood talking to you in the street for goodness knows how long, and forgotten all about his bronchitis. Oh, you authors, I believe you are every one like babies.' Richard smiled his gratification.

'Mr Larch, Mr Larch!' The roguish summons came after him when he was half-way up the street. He ran back and found her at the gate with her hands behind her.

'What have you forgotten?' she questioned. He could see her face but dimly in the twilight of the gas-lamps.

'I know – my umbrella,' he answered.

'Didn't I say you were all like – little children!' she said, as she whipped out the umbrella and gave it to him over the gate.

Anxious at once to add something original to the sum of Mr Aked's observations, he purposely chose a round-about route home, through the western parts of Fulham and past the Salisbury hotel. It seemed to him that the latent poetry of the suburbs arose like a beautiful vapour and filled these monotonous and squalid vistas with the scent and the colour of violets, leaving nothing common, nothing ignoble. In the upturned eyes of a shop-girl who went by on the arm of her lover he divined a passion as pure as that of Eugénie Grandet; on the wrinkled countenance of an older woman he beheld only the nobility of suffering; a youth who walked alone, smoking a cigarette, was a pathetic figure perhaps condemned to years of solitude in London. When there was no one else to see, he saw Adeline, – Adeline with her finger on her lips, Adeline angry with her uncle, Adeline pouring out tea, Adeline reaching down his hat from the peg, Adeline laughing at the gate. There was something about Adeline that . . . How the name suited her! . . . Her past life, judging from the hints she had given, must have been interesting. Perhaps that accounted for the charm which . . .

Then he returned to the book. He half regretted that Mr Aked should have a hand in it at all. He could do it himself. Just as plainly as if the idea had been his own, he saw the volume complete, felt the texture of the paper, admired the disposition of the titlepage, and the blue buckram binding; he scanned the table of contents, and carelessly eyed the brief introduction, which was, however, pregnant with meaning; chapter followed chapter in orderly, scientific fashion, and the last summed up the whole business in a few masterly and dignified sentences. Already, before a single idea had been reduced to words, 'The Psychology of the Suburbs' was finished! A unique work! Other authors had taken an isolated spot here or there in the suburbs and dissected it, but none had viewed them in their complex entirety; none had attempted to extract from their incoherence a coherent philosophy, to deal with them sympathetically as Mr Aked and himself had done – or rather were to do. None had suspected that the suburbs were a riddle, the answer to which was not undiscoverable. Ah, that secret, that key to the cipher! He saw it as it might be behind a succession of veils, flimsy obstructions which just then baffled his straining sight, but which he would rip and rend when the moment for effort came.

The same lofty sentiments occupied his brain the next morning. He paused in the knotting of his necktie, to look out of the window, seeking even in Raphael Street some fragment of that psychology of environment invented by Mr Aked. Nor did he search quite in vain. All the phenomena of humble life, hitherto witnessed daily without a second thought, now appeared to carry some mysterious meaning which was on the point of declaring itself. Friday, when the first formal conference was to occur, seemed distressingly distant. But he remembered that a very hard day's work, the casting and completing of a gigantic bill of costs, awaited him at the office, and he decided to throw himself into it without reserve; the time would pass more quickly.

XIII

Every solicitor's office has its great client, whose affairs, watchfully managed by the senior partner in person, take precedence of all else, and whom every member of the staff regards with a particular respect caught from the principals themselves. Messrs Curpet and Smythe were London agents to the tremendous legal firm of Pontifex, of Manchester, said to enjoy the largest practice in the midlands; and they were excusably proud of the fact. One of the first lessons that a new clerk learnt in the establishment at New Serjeant's Court was that, at no matter what expenditure of time and trouble, Pontifex business, comprising some scores of separate causes, must be transacted so irreproachably that old Mr Pontifex, by repute a terrible fellow, might never have cause of complaint. On those mornings, happily rare, when a querulous letter did by chance arrive from Manchester, the whole office trembled apprehensively, and any clerk likely to be charged with negligence began at once to consider the advisability of seeking a new situation.

The Pontifex bill of costs was made up annually in June. As the time drew near for presenting it, more and more clerks were pressed into its service, until at last everyone found himself engaged, in one way or another, upon this colossal account.

When Richard arrived at the office, he found the immense pile of white foolscap sheets upon his table, and next it the still higher pile of blue sheets forming the draft bill. All was finished except the checking of the figures and the final castings. As the cashier and accountant, he was ultimately responsible for this. He parcelled out the sheets, keeping the largest share for himself, and the work began. In every room there was a low muttering of figures, broken by an occasional oath when someone happened to lose the thread of an addition. The principals hovered about, full of solicitude and encouragement, and, according to custom on such occasions, lunch was served on the premises at the firm's expense. Richard continued to add while eating, keeping his head clear and seldom making a mistake; nothing existed for him but the column of pounds, shillings, and pence under his eyes.

The pile of finished sheets grew, and soon the office boys, commanded by Jenkins, were passing the earlier portion of the bill through the copying-press. As the hours went by, the helpers from other departments, no longer required, went back to their own neglected duties, and Richard did the last additions alone. At length the bill was absolutely finished, and he carried it himself to the stationer's to be sewed. In half an hour it came back, and he laid it ceremoniously before Mr Curpet. The grand total went round the office, leaping from lip to lip like the result of an important parliamentary poll. It was higher than in any previous year by nearly a thousand pounds. Each of the clerks took a personal pride in its bigness, and secretly determined to petition for an increase of salary at the first opportunity. They talked together in groups, discussing details, while a comfortable lassitude spread from room to room.

Richard stood by the open window, absently watching the pigeons and the cleaners at the Law Courts opposite. In a corner an office boy, new to his work, was stamping envelopes with slow precision. Jenkins, with one foot on a table, was tying a shoe lace. It had struck six ten minutes ago, and everyone was gone except Mr Smythe, whose departure Jenkins awaited with impatience. The hot day subsided slowly to a serene and lovely evening, and the customary noises of the Strand ascended to Richard like the pastoral hum of a valley to a dweller on a hill, not breaking but rather completing the stillness of the hour. Gradually his brain freed itself from the obsession of figures, though he continued to muse vaguely over the bill, which had just been posted. It would certainly be settled by cheque within a week, for Messrs Pontifex were invariably prompt. That cheque, which he himself would enter and pay into the bank, amounted to as much as he could earn in twenty years, if he remained a clerk. He tried to imagine the scene in which, at some future date, he would give Mr Curpet notice of his intention to resign his position, explaining that he preferred to support himself by literature. The ineffable sweetness of such a triumph! Could he ever realise it? He could, he must; the alternative of eternal clerkship was not to be endured. His glance fell on Jenkins. That poor, gay, careless, vulgar animal would always be a clerk. The thought filled him with commiseration, and also with pride. Fancy Jenkins writing a book called 'The Pyschology of the Suburbs'!

'I'm going to smoke,' Jenkins said; 'be blowed to Bertie dear.' (Mrs Smythe had once addressed her husband in the office as 'Bertie dear,' and thenceforth that had been his name among the staff.) Richard made no answer. When a minute later Jenkins, discreetly directing his puffs to the open window, asked him for the titles of one or two of Zola's novels in English, and their price, he gave the required information without turning round and in a preoccupied tone. It was his wish at that moment to appear dreamy. Perhaps a hint of the intellectual difference between them would suggest itself even to Jenkins. Suddenly a voice that seemed to be Mr Smythe's came from the other side of the glass partition which separated the room from the general corridor.

'Jenkins, what the devil do you mean by smoking in the office?' The pipe vanished instantly, and Jenkins faced the accuser in some confusion, only to find that he had been victimised. It was Mr Aked.

'You're as gassy as ever, I see,' Jenkins said with a shade of annoyance. Mr Aked laughed, and then began to cough badly, bending forward with flushed cheeks.

'Surely you shouldn't have left the house to-day,' Richard said, alarmed.

'Why not?' The retort was almost fierce.

'You're not fit.'

'Fiddlesticks! I've only got a bit of a cough.'

Richard wondered what he had called for.

Jenkins began to discuss with him the shortcomings of Mr Smythe as an employer, and when that fruitful subject was exhausted there was silence.

'Coming home?' Mr Aked asked Richard, who at once prepared to leave.

'By the way, Larch, how's the mash?' Jenkins wore his archest manner.

'What mash?'

'Why, the girl you said you were going to see yesterday afternoon.'

'I never said——' Richard began, looking nervously towards Mr Aked.

'Oh, no, of course not. Do you know, Mr Aked, he's begun his little games with the women. These fellows from the country – so shy and all that – they're regular cautions when you come to know them.' But Mr Aked made no response.

'I was thinking you might as well come down to-morrow night instead of Friday,' he said quietly to Richard, who had busied himself with the locking of a safe.

'To-morrow? Certainly, I shall be very glad,' Richard answered. Evidently Mr Aked was as eager as himself to make a beginning of the book. No doubt that was why he had called. Surely, together they would accomplish something notable!

Jenkins had climbed on a lofty stool. He gave vent to a whistle, and the other two observed that his features were twisted into an expression of delirious mirth.

'Aha! aha!' he grinned, looking at Richard. 'I begin to perceive. You're after the pretty niece, eh, Master Larch? And a nice plump little thing she is, too! She came here once to fetch uncle home.'

Mr Aked sprang instantly forward and cuffed Jenkins' ear.

'It's not the first time I've had to do that, nor the second,' he said. 'I suppose you never will learn to behave yourself.' Jenkins could easily have thrashed the old man – he really looked old to-day – and no consideration for the latter's age would have restrained him from doing so, had not the habit of submission acquired during those years when Mr Aked ruled the outer office proved stronger than his rage. As it was, he took up a safe position behind the stool and contented himself with words.

'You're a beauty you are!' he began. 'How's the red-haired A.B.C. girl getting on? You know, the one that lost her place at the Courts' restaurant through you. If she hadn't been a fool, she'd have brought an action for breach of promise. And how many more are there? I wonder——'

Mr Aked made an uncertain dart after him, but he vanished through the doorway, only to encounter Mr Smythe. With a rather servile ''d afternoon, sir,' to the latter, Mr Aked walked rapidly out of the office.

'What the devil are you all up to?' Mr Smythe inquired crossly. 'Is Aked after money, Larch?'

'Not at all, Mr Smythe. He only called to see me.'

'You are a friend of his, are you?'

'Well, I know him.'

'H'm! Jenkins, come and take a letter.'

As Richard hurried down into the court, he felt exceedingly angry with Mr Aked. Why could not the man be more dignified? Everyone seemed to treat him with contempt, and the cause was not altogether obscure. He had no dignity. Richard felt personally aggrieved.

Neither of them spoke of the recent incident as they walked down to the Temple station. Mr Aked, indeed, said nothing; a fit of coughing occupied him. Somehow Richard's faith in 'The Psychology of the Suburbs' had lessened a little during the last half-hour.

XIV

'Is that you, Mr Larch?'

He indistinctly made out Adeline's head and bust above him. Her white apron was pressed against the bannisters, as with extended arms and hands grasping the stair-rail she leaned over to see who was below.

'It is, Miss Aked,' he answered. 'The door was open, so I walked in. Is anything wrong?'

'I've just sent Lottie out for the doctor. Uncle is very ill. I wish you'd see that he comes at once. It's in the Fulham Road, a little to the left – you'll notice the red lamp.'

As Richard ran out, he met the doctor, a youngish man with a Scots face and grey hair, hurrying down the street, the servant-girl breathless in the rear.

'Master was took ill last night, sir,' the latter said, in answer to Richard's question. 'Pneumonia, the doctor says as it is, and something else, and there's coming a nurse to-night. Master has attacks of it, sir – he can't get his breath.'

He stood in the passage, uncertain what to do; the doctor had already gone upstairs.

'It must be very serious,' he murmured.

'Yes, sir.' Lottie began to whimper. Richard said he would call again later to make inquiries, and presently discovered himself in Fulham Road, walking slowly towards Putney.

Mr Aked's case was hopeless; of that Richard felt sure. The man must be getting on in years, and his frame, not constitutionally vigorous, had doubtless been fatally weakened by long-continued carelessness. What a strange creature of whims and enthusiasms he was! Although there could be no question as to his age, Richard never regarded him as more than a few years older than himself. He had none of the melancholy, the circumspection, the fixity of view, the prudent tendency towards compromise, the serene contented apathy, which usually mark his time of life. He was still delicately susceptible to new influences, his ideals were as fluid as Richard's own. Life had taught him scarcely anything, and least of all sagacity and a dignified carriage. He was the typical bachelor, whose deeper feelings have never been stirred. Did regrets for a possibly happier past, shadows of dead faces, the memory of kisses, ever ruffle his equanimity? Richard thought not. He must always have lived in the present. But he was an artist: though somehow the man had descended in his estimation, Richard clung to that. He possessed imagination and he possessed intellect, and he could fuse them together. Yet he had been a failure. Viewed in certain lights, Richard admitted he was a pitiful figure. What was his true history? Richard felt instinctively that none could answer that question, even in outline, except Mr Aked, and suddenly he discerned that the man's nature, apparently frank to immodesty, had its own reserves, the existence of which few ever suspected. And when the worst was said, Mr Aked possessed originality; in an incongruous way he still retained the naïve graces of youthfulness; he was inspiring, and had exerted influences for which Richard could not but be grateful.

'The Psychology of the Suburbs' had receded swiftly into the background, a beautiful, impossible idea! Richard knew now that it could never have been carried out. A little progress would have been made, and then, as difficulties increased, both he and Mr Aked would have tacitly abandoned their enterprise. They were very much alike, he thought, and the fancied similarity pleased him. Perhaps at some future time he might himself carry the undertaking to completion, in which case he would dedicate his book to the memory of Mr Aked. He did not regret that the dream of the last few days was ended. It had been very enjoyable, but the awakening, since according to his present wisdom it must have occurred sooner or later, was less unpleasant now than it could have been at any more advanced stage. Moreover, it was pleasant to dream of the dream.

Mr Aked was dying: he knew it from Adeline's tone. Poor Adeline! To whom would she turn? She had implied that the only relatives for whom she cared, these being on her mother's side, were in America. From whom would she seek assistance? Who would conduct the formalities of the funeral, and the testamentary business, such as it was? His loathing for funerals seemed to have vanished and he was not without hope that Adeline, though their acquaintance was of the shortest, might engage his help for her helplessness. And after the funeral, what would she do? Since she would probably have enough to live upon, she might elect to remain where she was. In which case he would visit her now and then of an evening. Her imminent loneliness gave her a pathetic charm, and he made haste to draw a picture of himself and her on either side of the fireplace talking familiarly while she knitted or sewed.

Yes, he was actually a grown man, and entitled to his romances. He might eventually fall in love with her, having discovered in her character rare qualities now unsuspected. It was improbable, but not impossible, and he had, in fact, already glanced at the contingency several times before. Oh for a passion, a glorious infatuation, even if it ended in disaster and ruin! The difficulty was that Adeline fell short of the ideal lover. That virginal abstraction was to have been an artist of some sort, absolutely irreligious, broad in social views, the essence of refinement, with a striking but not necessarily beautiful face, soft-spoken, and isolated – untrammelled by friends. Adeline was no artist; he feared she might be a regular attendant at chapel and painfully orthodox as to the sexual relations. Was she refined? Had she a striking face? He said Yes, twice. Her voice was low and full of pretty modulations. Soon, perhaps, she would be alone in the world. If only she had been an artist . . . That deficiency, he was afraid, would prove fatal to any serious attachment. Still, it would be good to visit her.

He was crossing Putney Bridge. Night had fallen, and the full brilliant moon showed a narrow stream crawling between two broad flats of mud. Just below the bridge a barge lay at anchor; the silhouette of a man moved leisurely about on it, and then a boat detached itself from the stem of the barge and dropped down river into darkness. On the bridge buses and waggons rattled noisily. Young men with straw hats and girls in white blouses and black skirts passed to and fro in pairs, some chattering, some silent. The sight of these couples gave Richard an idea for the abandoned 'Psychology of the Suburbs.' What if Mr Aked recovered? He remembered his sister telling him that their grandfather had survived after having been three times surrendered to death by the doctors. 'The Psychology of the Suburbs' began to attract him again. It might come to completion, if Mr Aked lived, and then . . . But what about those evenings with the lonely Adeline? The two vistas of the future clashed with and obscured each other, and he was overcome by vague foreboding. He saw Mr Aked struggling for breath in the mean suburban bedroom, and Adeline powerless at his side. The pathos of her position became intolerable.

When he got back to Carteret Street, it was she who came to the door.

'How is he?'

'About the same. The nurse has come. She told me to go to bed at once, but I don't feel as if I wanted to sleep. You will sit down a little?'

She took the rocking-chair, and leaning back with a gesture of lassitude rocked gently; her white face, with red eyes and drooping eyelids, gave sign of excessive fatigue, and on her lips there was a gloomy pout. After she had described Mr Aked's condition in some detail and told what the doctor had said, they sat silent for a while in that tense atmosphere which seems to stifle vitality in a house of dangerous sickness. Overhead the nurse moved about, making the window rattle softly now and then.

'You have known uncle a long time, haven't you?'

'Not at all,' Richard answered. 'It's a very funny thing, but though I seem to know him quite well, I've not met him half a dozen times in my life. I saw him first about a year ago, and then I met him again the other day at the British Museum, and after we'd had dinner together we were just like old friends.'

'I certainly thought from what he said that you *were* old friends. Uncle has so few friends. Except one or two neighbours I do believe you are the first person that has ever called at this house since I came to live here.'

'At any rate, we have soon got to know each other,' said Richard, smiling. 'It isn't a week since you asked me if my name was Larch.' She returned the smile, though rather mechanically.

'Perhaps my mistake about your being an old friend of Uncle Aked's explains that,' she said.

'Well, we won't bother about explaining it; there it is, and if I can help you in any way just now, you must tell me.'

'Thank you, I will.' She said it with perfect simplicity. Richard was conscious of a scarcely perceptible thrill.

'You must have had an awful time last night, all alone,' he said.

'Yes, but I was too annoyed to feel upset.'

'Annoyed?'

'Because uncle has brought it all on himself by carelessness. I do think it's a shame!' She stopped rocking, and sat up, her face full of serious protest.

'He's not the sort of man to take care of himself. He never thought——'

'That's just it. He should have thought, at his age. If he dies, he will practically have killed himself, yes, killed himself. There's no excuse, going out as he did, in spite of all I said. Fancy him coming downstairs last Sunday in the state he was, and then going out on Monday, though it *was* warm!'

'Well, we'll hope he will get better, and it may be a lesson to him.'

'Hark! What was that?' She sprang to her feet apprehensively and listened, her breast pulsing beneath the tight black bodice and her startled inquiring eyes fixed on Richard's. A very faint tinkle came from the rear of the house.

'Perhaps the front-door bell,' he suggested.

'Of course. How silly of me! I fancied . . . Who can it be at this time?' She went softly into the passage. Richard heard the door open, and then a woman's voice, which somehow seemed familiar, –

'How is Mr Aked to-night? Your servant told our servant that he was ill, and I felt anxious.'

'Oh!' Adeline exclaimed, discomposed for a moment, as it seemed to Richard; then she went on coldly, 'Uncle is about the same, thank you,' and almost immediately closed the door.

'A person to inquire about uncle,' she said to Richard, with a peculiar intonation, on re-entering the room. Then, just as he was saying that he must go, there was a knock on the ceiling and she flew away again. Richard waited in the passage till she came downstairs.

'It's nothing. I thought he was dying! Oh!' and she began to cry freely and openly, without attempting to wipe her eyes.

Richard gazed hard at the apron string loosely encircling her waist; from that white line her trembling bust rose like a bud from its calyx, and below it the black dress flowed over her broad hips in gathered folds; he had never seen a figure so exquisite, and the beauty of it took a keener poignancy from their solitude in the still, anxious night – the nurse and the sick man were in another sphere.

'Hadn't you better go to bed?' he said. 'You must be tired out and over-excited.' How awkward and conventional the words sounded!

XV

In Adeline's idiosyncrasy there was a subtle, elusive suggestion of singularity, of unexpectedness, which Richard in spite of himself found very alluring, and he correctly attributed it, in some degree, to the peculiar circumstances of her early life, an account of which, with characteristic quaintness, she had given him at their second meeting.

The posthumous child of Richard Aked's brother, Adeline, who had no recollection of her mother, lived at first with her maternal grandparents and two uncles. She slept alone at the top of the house, and when she arose in the morning from the big bed with its red curtains and yellow tassels, she always ran to the window. Immediately below here were the leads which roofed the great projecting windows of the shop. It was her practice at night to scatter crumbs on the leads, and sometimes she would be early enough to watch the sparrows pecking them; more often all the crumbs had vanished while she was yet asleep. The Square never failed to interest her in the morning. In the afternoon it seemed torpid and morose; but before dinner, more especially on Saturdays and Mondays, it was gaily alert – full of canvas-covered stalls, and horses and carts, and heaped piles of vegetables, and pigs grunting amidst straw, and rough rosy-faced men, their trousers tied at the knees with string, who walked about heavily, cracking whips. These things arrived mysteriously, before the sun, and in the afternoon they dwindled imperceptibly away; the stalls were unthatched, the carts jolted off one by one, and the pigs departed squeaking, until at five o'clock the littered Square was left deserted and forlorn. Now and again a new stall, unfolding vivid white canvas, stood out brightly amid its soiled companions; then Adeline would run downstairs to her favourite uncle, who had breakfast at 7.30 so that he might be in charge of the shop while the rest were at table: 'Uncle Mark, Uncle Mark, there is a new stall up at the top of the Square, near the New Inn!' 'Perhaps it is only an old one with its face washed,' Uncle Mark would say; and Adeline, raising her right shoulder, would put her head on it and laugh, screwing up her eyes.

  In those days she was like a little Puritan girl, with her plain frocks and prim gait. Her black hair, confined by a semicircular comb which stretched from ear to ear over the top of her head, was brushed straight away from her forehead, and fell across the entire width of her shoulders in glossy, wavy lines. Her grey eyes were rather large, except when she laughed, and they surveyed people with a frank, inquiring look which frightened some of the commercial travellers who came into the shop and gave her threepenny bits; it seemed as if all one's secret shames stood revealed to that artless gaze. Her nose was short and flattened, but her mouth happened to be perfect, of exactly the classic form and size, with delectable lips half hiding the small white teeth.

To her the house appeared to be of immense proportions; she had been told that once, before she was born, it was three houses. Certainly it possessed more than the usual number of staircases, and one of these, with the single room to which it gave access, was always closed. From the Square, the window of the disused chamber, obscured and bare, contrasted strangely with the clear panes, white blinds, and red pads of the others. This room was next to her own, the two staircases running parallel; and the thought of its dread emptiness awed her at nights. One Saturday night in bed she discovered that grandma, who had been plaiting her hair for Sunday, had left a comb sticking in it. She called aloud to grandma, to Uncle Mark, to Uncle Luke, in vain. None of them came to her; but she distinctly heard an answering cry from the shut room. She ceased to call, and lay fearfully quiet for a while; then it was morning, and the comb had slipped out of her hair and down into the bed.

Beneath the houses were many cellars. One served for kitchen, and Adeline had a swing there, hung from a beam; two others were larders; a fourth held coal, and in a fifth ashes were thrown. There were yet two more under the shop, to be reached by a separate flight of stone steps. Uncle Mark went down those steps every afternoon to turn on the gas, but he would never allow Adeline to go with him. Grandma, indeed, was very cross if, when the door leading to the steps happened to be open, Adeline approached within a yard of it. Often, chattering to the shop-girls, who at quiet times of the day clustered round the stove with their sewing, she would suddenly think of the cellars below, and her heart would seem to stop.

If the shutters were up, the shop was even more terribly mysterious than either the cellars or the disused room. On Sunday afternoons, when grandpa snored behind a red and yellow handkerchief in the breakfast-room, it was necessary for Adeline to go through the shop and up the show-room staircase, in order to reach the drawing-room, because to get to the house staircase would involve disturbing the sleeper. How strange the shop looked as she hurried timorously across! A dim twilight, worse than total darkness, filtered through the cracks of the shutters, showing faintly the sallow dust-sheets which covered the merinos and the chairs on the counters, and she always reached the show-room, which had two large, unobstructed windows, with a sob of relief. Very few customers were asked into the show-room; Adeline employed it on weekdays as a nursery; here she nursed her dolls, flew kites, and read 'Little Wideawake,' a book given to her by a commercial traveller; there was a cheval glass near the front window in which she contemplated herself long and seriously.

She never had the companionship of other children, nor did she desire it. Other children, she understood, were rude and dirty; although Uncle Mark and Uncle Luke taught in the Sunday-school, and grandpa had once actually been superintendent, she was not allowed to go there, simply because the children were rude and dirty. But she went to morning chapel, sitting alone with grandpa on the red cushions of the broad pew, that creaked every time she moved; Uncle Mark and Uncle Luke sat away up in the gallery with the rude and dirty Sunday-school children; grandma seldom went to chapel; the ministers called to see her instead. Once to her amazement Uncle Luke had ascended the pulpit stairs, looking just as if he was walking in his sleep, and preached. It seemed so strange, and afterwards the religious truths which she had been taught somehow lost their awfulness and some of their reality. On Sunday evenings she celebrated her own private service, in which she was preacher, choir, organist, and congregation. Her extempore prayers were the secret admiration of grandma, who alone heard them. Adeline stayed up for supper on Sundays. When the meal was over, grandpa opened the big Bible, and in his rich, heavy voice read that Shem begat Arphaxad and Arphaxad begat Salah and Salah begat Eber and Eber begat Pelag, and about the Ammonites and the Jebusites and the Canaanites and the Moabites; and then they knelt, and he prayed for them that rule over us, and widows and orphans; and at the word 'orphans,' grandma, who didn't kneel like the others but sat upright in her rocking-chair with one hand over her eyes, would say 'Amen, Amen,' under her breath. And after it was all over Adeline would choose whether Uncle Mark or Uncle Luke should carry her to bed.

Grandpa died, and then grandma, and Aunt Grace (who was not an aunt at all, but a cousin) came to stay with Adeline and her uncles, and one day the shutters of the shop were put up and not taken down again. Adeline learnt that Uncle Mark and Uncle Luke were going a long way off, to America, and that she was to live in future with Aunt Grace in a large and splendid house full of coloured pictures and statues and books. It seemed odd that Aunt Grace, whose dresses were rather shabby, should have a finer house than grandpa's, until Uncle Mark explained that the house did not really belong to Aunt Grace; Aunt Grace merely kept it in order for a rich young gentleman who had fifteen servants.

When she had recovered from the parting with her uncles, Adeline accepted the change with docility. Long inured as she was to spiritual solitude (for the closest friendship that can exist between a child and an adult comprises little more than an affectionate tolerance on either side, and certainly knows nothing of those intimate psychic affinities which attract child to child or man to man), she could not, indeed, have easily found much hardship in the conditions of her new life. One matter troubled her at first, namely, that Aunt Grace never prayed or read the Bible or went to chapel; nor, so far as Adeline knew, did anyone else at the Abbey. But she soon became reconciled to this state of things. For a time she continued to repeat her prayers; then the habit ceased.

The picture-gallery, of which she had heard a great deal, fascinated her at once. It was a long but not very lofty apartment, receiving daylight from a hidden source, hung with the finest examples of the four great Italian schools which flourished during the first half of the sixteenth century: the Venetian, a revel of colour; the Roman, dignified and even sedate; the Florentine, nobly grandiose; and the school of Parma, mysteriously delicate. Opportunity serving, she spent much of her time here, talking busily to the madonnas, the Christs, the martyred saints, the monarchs, the knights, the lovely ladies, and all the naïve mediæval crowd, giving each of them a part in her own infantile romances. When she grew older, she copied – who shall say whether consciously or unconsciously? – the attitudes and gestures of the women; and perhaps in time there passed into Adeline, by some ineffable channel, at least a portion of their demure grace and contented quietude. There were pictures also in the square library, examples of quite modern English and French work, sagaciously chosen by one whose critical faculty had descended to him through four generations of collectors; but Adeline had no eyes for these. The books, however, gorgeous prisoners in glass, were her good friends, though she might never touch them, and though the narrow, conventional girl's education assiduously bestowed upon her by her aunt in person, stifled rather than fostered curiosity with regard to their contents.

When Adeline was about nineteen, her guardian became engaged to be married to a middle-aged farmer, a tenant of the Abbey, who made it clear that in espousing Aunt Grace he was not eager to espouse Aunt Grace's *protégée* also. A serious question arose as to her future. She had only one other relative in England, Mr Aked, and she passively accepted his timely suggestion that she should go to London and keep house for him.

XVI

On the Wednesday evening Richard took tea at the Crabtree, so that he might go down by train to Parson's Green direct from Charing Cross. The coffee-room was almost empty of customers; and Miss Roberts, who appeared to be in attendance there, was reading in the 'cosy corner,' an angle of the room furnished with painted mirrors and a bark bench of fictitious rusticity.

'What are you doing up here?' he asked, when she brought his meal. 'Aren't you cashier downstairs any longer?'

'Oh, yes,' she said, 'I should just think I was. But the girl that waits in this room, Miss Pratt, has her half-holiday on Wednesdays, and I come here, and the governor takes my place downstairs. I do it to oblige him. He's a gentleman, he is. *That* polite! I have my half-holiday on Fridays.'

'Well, if you've nothing else to do, what do you say to pouring out my tea for me?'

'Can't you pour it out yourself? Poor thing!' She smiled pityingly, and began to pour out the tea.

'Sit down,' Richard suggested.

'No, thank you,' she said. 'There! If it isn't sweet enough, you can put another lump in yourself;' and she disappeared behind the screen which hid the food-lift.

Presently he summoned her to make out his check. He was debating whether to tell her that Mr Aked was ill. Perhaps if he did so she might request to be informed how the fact concerned herself. He decided to say nothing, and was the more astonished when she began:

'Did you know Mr Aked was very ill?'

'Yes. Who told you?'

'Why, I live near him, a few doors away – didn't I tell you once? – and their servant told ours.'

'Told your servant?'

'Yes,' said Miss Roberts, reddening a little, and with an inflection which meant, 'I suppose you thought *my* family wouldn't have a servant!'

'Oh!' He stopped a moment and then an idea came to him. 'It must have been you who called last night to inquire!' He wondered why Adeline had been so curt with her.

'Were you there then?'

'Oh, yes. I know the Akeds pretty well.'

'The doctor says he'll not get better. What do you think?'

'I'm afraid it's a bad lookout.'

'Very sad for poor Miss Aked, isn't it?' she said, and something in the tone made Richard look up at her.

'Yes,' he agreed.

'Of course you like her?'

'I scarcely know her – it's the old man I know,' he replied guardedly.

'Well, if you ask me, I think she's a bit stand-offish.'

'Perhaps that's only her manner.'

'You've noticed it too, have you?'

'Not a bit. I've really seen very little of her.'

'Going down again to-night?'

'I may do.'

Nothing had passed between Adeline and himself as to his calling that day, but when he got to Carteret Street she evidently accepted his presence as a matter of course, and he felt glad. There was nothing in her demeanour to recall the scene of the previous night. He did not stay long. Mr Aked's condition was unchanged. Adeline had watched by him all day, while the nurse slept, and now she confessed to an indisposition.

'My bones ache,' she said, with an attempt to laugh, 'and I feel miserable, though under the circumstances there's nothing strange in that.'

He feared she might be sickening towards influenza, caught from her uncle, but said nothing, lest he should alarm her without cause. The next day, however, his apprehension was justified. On his way to the house in the evening he met the doctor at the top of Carteret Street and stopped him.

'You're a friend of Mr Aked's, eh?' the doctor said, examining Richard through his gold-rimmed spectacles. 'Well, go and do what you can. Miss Aked is down with the influenza now, but I don't think it will be a severe attack if she takes care. The old fellow's state is serious. You see, he has no constitution, though perhaps that's scarcely a disadvantage in these cases; but when it comes to double basic pneumonia, with fever, and cardiac complications, pulse 140, respiration 40, temperature 103 to 104, there's not a great deal of chance. I've got a magnificent nurse, though, and she'll have her hands full. We ought really to send for another one, especially as Miss Aked wants looking after too. . . . Bless you,' he went on, in answer to a question from Richard, 'I can't say. I injected strychnia this morning, and that has given relief, but he may die during the night. On the other hand he may recover. By the way, they seem to have no relations, except a cousin of Mr Aked's who lives in the north. I've wired to her. Good evening. See what you can do. I'm due in my surgery in two minutes.'

Richard introduced himself to the nurse, explained that he had seen the doctor, and asked if he could render assistance. She was a slender girl of about twenty-three, with dark, twinkling eyes and astonishingly small white ears; her blue uniform, made of the same print as a servant's morning-dress, fitted without a crease, and her immense apron was snowy. On one linen cuff was a stain; she noticed this while talking to Richard, and adroitly reversed the wristband under his very gaze.

'I suppose you know the Akeds pretty well?' she questioned.

'Well, pretty well,' he answered.

'Do you know any friends of theirs, women, who happen to live near?'

'I feel fairly sure they have practically no acquaintances. I have never met any people here.'

'It is very awkward, now that Miss Aked is taken ill.'

The mention of Adeline gave him an opportunity to make more particular inquiries as to her condition.

'There is nothing to be afraid of,' the nurse said, 'only she must stay in bed and keep quite quiet.'

'I fancied last night she looked ill,' he said sagely.

'You were here last night?'

'Yes, and the night before.'

'Oh! I wasn't aware——' The nurse stopped a moment. 'Pardon me, if I am indiscreet, but are you engaged to Miss Aked?'

'No,' said Richard shortly, uncertain whether or not he was blushing. The nurse's eyes twinkled, but otherwise her impassive gravity suffered no diminishment. 'Not at all,' he added. 'I am merely a friend, anxious to do anything I can.'

'I will get you to do some marketing for me,' she decided suddenly. 'The maid is sitting with Mr Aked – he is a little easier for the moment – and Miss Aked, I think, is asleep. If I give you a list, can you discover the shops? I am quite ignorant of this neighbourhood.'

Richard thought he could discover the shops.

'In the meantime I will have a bath. I have had no rest worth mentioning for twenty-four hours, and I want freshening up. Don't come back for twenty minutes, or there will be no one to let you in. Stay, I will give you the latch-key.' It was attached to her chatelaine.

Equipped with written orders and a sovereign, he went out. Though he was away barely a quarter of an hour, she was dressed and downstairs again when he came in, her face as radiant as if she had just risen. She counted the change, and checked the different purchases with the list. Richard had made no mistakes.

'Thank you,' she said formally. He had expected a little praise.

'Is there anything else I can do?' he asked, determined not to weary in good works, however coldly his efforts were received.

'I think you might sit with Mr Aked for a while,' she said; 'I must positively give some attention to Miss Aked, and half an hour's rest would not harm me. See, there are some slippers; would you mind taking off your boots and putting those on instead? Thank you. You may talk to Mr Aked if he talks to you, and let him hold your hand – he'll probably want to. Let him have just a sip of the brandy and milk I will give you, whenever he asks for it. Don't mind if he grumbles at everything you do. Try to soothe him. Remember he is very seriously ill. Shall I take you upstairs?'

She looked at Richard and then at the door; and Richard, hesitating for a fraction of a second, stepped past her to open it. He managed it awkwardly because he had never done such a thing for a lady in his life, nor could he quite understand what mysterious prompting had led him to be so punctilious now. The nurse bowed an acknowledgment and preceded him to the sick-room. He felt as a student feels just before the examination papers are handed round.

A smell of linseed escaped from the bedroom as the nurse pushed open the door.

'Stay outside a moment,' she said to Richard. He could see the grate, on which a kettle was singing over a small fire. In front of the fire was a board, with a large bowl and spoon, and some pieces of linen. Then he was conscious of nothing but a loud sound of rapid, painful breathing, accompanied by moans and a strange rattling which came to his ears with perturbing distinctness. He knew nothing of sickness beyond what people had told him, and these phenomena inspired him with physical dread. He wished to run away.

'A friend of yours is coming to sit with you, Mr Aked – you know Mr Larch,' he heard the nurse say; she was evidently busy about the bed. 'You can go now, Lottie,' she went on to the servant. 'Wash up the things I have put in the sink, and then off to bed.'

Richard waited with painful expectancy for the voice of Mr Aked.

'Larch – did you say – why – didn't he come – before?' The tones were less unnatural than he had anticipated, but it seemed that only by the exercise of a desperate ingenuity could the speaker interject the fragments of a sentence here and there between his hurrying gasps.

Then the servant went downstairs.

'Come in, Mr Larch,' the nurse called pleasantly.

The patient, supported by pillows, was sitting upright in bed, and as Richard entered he looked towards the door with the expression of an unarmed man on the watch for an assassin. His face was drawn and duskily pale, but on each cheek burned a red flush; at every cruel inspiration the nostrils dilated widely, and the shoulders were raised in a frenzied effort to fill the embarrassed lungs.

'Well, Mr Aked,' Richard greeted him, 'here I am, you see.'

He made no reply beyond a weak nod, and signed to the nurse for the feeding-cup of brandy and milk, which she held to his mouth. Richard was afraid he might not be able to stay in the room, and marvelled that the nurse could be unmoved and cheerful in the midst of this piteous altercation with death. Was she blind to the terror in the man's eyes?

'You had better sit here, Mr Larch,' she said quietly, pointing to a chair by the bedside. 'Here is the drink; hold the cup – so. Ring this bell if you want me for anything.' Then she noiselessly disappeared.

No sooner had he sat down than Mr Aked seized his shoulder for support, and each movement of the struggling frame communicated itself to Richard's body. Richard suddenly received a boundless respect for the nurse, who had watched whole nights by this tortured organism on the bed. Somehow existence began to assume for him a new and larger aspect; he felt that till that moment he had been going through the world with his eyes closed; life was sublimer, more terrible, than he had thought. He abased himself before all doctors and nurses and soldiers in battle; they alone tasted the true savour of life.

Art was a very little thing.

Presently Mr Aked breathed with slightly less exertion, and he appeared to doze for a few moments now and then, though Richard could scarcely believe that any semblance of sleep was possible to a man in his condition.

'Adeline?' he questioned once.

'She's getting on fine,' Richard said soothingly. 'Would you like a sip?'

He put his grey lips clumsily round the lip of the cup, drank, and then pushed the vessel away with a gesture of irritation.

The windows were open, but the air was perfectly still, and the gas burnt without a tremor between the windows and the door.

'I'm stifled,' the patient gasped. 'Are they – doing – all they can – for me?' Richard tried to reassure him.

'It's all over – with me – Larch – I can't – keep it up long – I'm going – going – they'll have to try – something else.'

His lustrous eyes were fastened on Richard with an appealing gaze. Richard turned away.

'I'm frightened – I thought I shouldn't be – but I am. Doctor suggested parson – it's not that – I said no . . . Do you think – I'm dying?'

'Not a bit,' said Richard.

'That's a lie – I'm off . . . It's a big thing, – death – everyone's afraid – of it – at last . . . Instinct! . . . Shows there's something – awful behind it.'

If Richard had been murdering the man, he could not have had a sharper sense of guilt than at that moment oppressed him.

Mr Aked continued to talk, but with a growing incoherence which gradually passed into delirium. Richard looked at his watch. Only thirty minutes had slipped by, and yet he felt as if his shoulder had suffered the clutch of that hot hand since before the beginning of time! Again he experienced the disconcerting sensation of emotional horizons suddenly widened.

People were walking down the street; they talked and laughed. How incongruously mirthful and careless their voices sounded! Perhaps they had never watched by a sick-bed, never listened to the agonised breathing of a pneumonia patient. That incessant frantic intake of air! It exasperated him. If it did not stop soon, he should go mad. He stared at the gas-flame, and the gas-flame grew larger, larger, till he could see nothing else. . . . Then, after a long while, surely the breathing was more difficult! There was a reverberating turmoil in the man's chest which shook the bed. Could Richard have been asleep, or what? He started up; but Mr Aked clung desperately to him, raising his shoulders higher and higher in the struggle to inhale, and leaning forward till he was bent almost double. Richard hesitated, and then struck the bell. It seemed as if the nurse would never come.

The door opened softly.

'I'm afraid he is much worse,' Richard said to the nurse, striving to cover his agitation. She looked at Mr Aked.

'Perhaps you had better fetch the doctor.'

When he returned, Mr Aked was lying back unconscious.

'Of course the doctor can do nothing now,' said the nurse, calmly answering the question in his eyes. 'He'll never speak any more.'

'But Miss Aked?'

'It can't be helped. I shall say nothing to her till morning.'

'Then she won't see him?'

'Certainly not. It would be madness for her to leave her bed.'

The doctor arrived, and the three talked quietly together about the alarming prevalence of influenza at that time of the year, and the fatal results of carelessness.

'I tell you honestly,' the doctor said, 'I'm so overworked that I should be quite satisfied to step into my coffin and not wake again. I've had three 3 A.M. midwifery cases this week – forceps, chloroform, and the whole bag of tricks – on the top of all this influenza, and I'm about sick of it. That's the worst of our trade; it comes in lumps. What do you say, nurse?'

XVII

The nurse suggested that Richard should remain at Carteret Street for the rest of the night, using the sofa in the sitting-room. Contrary to his expectation, he slept well and dreamlessly for several hours, and woke up refreshed and energetic. The summer sun was dispersing a light mist. One thought occupied his mind, – Adeline's isolation and need of succour. Mentally he enveloped her with tender solicitude; and the prospect of giving her instant aid, and so earning her gratitude, contributed to a mood of vigorous cheerfulness to which his sorrow for Mr Aked's death formed but a vague and distant background.

No one seemed to be stirring. He washed luxuriously in the little scullery, and then, silently unbolting the front door, went out for a walk.

It was just six o'clock, and above the weazen trees which line either side of Carteret Street the sparrows were noisily hilarious. As he strode along in the fresh, sunny air, his fancy pictured scene after scene between himself and Adeline in which he rendered a man's help and she offered a woman's gratitude. He determined to take upon himself all the arrangements for the funeral, and looked forward pleasurably to activities from which under different circumstances he would have shrunk with dismay. He thought of Adeline's aunt or cousin, distant in the north, and wondered whether she or any other relatives, if such existed, would present themselves; he hoped that Adeline might be forced to rely solely on him. A milkboy who passed with his rattling cans observed Richard talking rapidly to no visible person, and turned round to stare.

When he got back to the house, he noticed that the blinds had been drawn in the sitting-room. Lottie, the chubby-armed servant, was cleaning the step; her eyes were red with crying.

'Is nurse up yet?' he asked her.

'Yes, sir, she's in the kitchen,' the girl whimpered.

He sprang over the wet step into the passage. As his glance fell on the stairs leading up to the room where lay the body of Mr Aked, separated from the unconscious Adeline only by a gimcrack wall of lath and plaster, an uncomfortable feeling of awe took hold of him. Death was very incurable, and he had been assisting at a tragedy. How unreal and distorted seemed the events of a few hours before! He had a curious sense of partnership in shame, as if he and the nurse and the doctor had last night done Adeline an injury and were conspiring to hide their sin. What would she say when she knew that her uncle was dead? What would be her plans? It occurred to him now that she would of course act quite independently of himself; it was ridiculous to suppose that he, comparatively a stranger, could stand to her in the place of kith and kin; he had been dreaming. He was miserably disheartened.

He made his way to the kitchen, and, pushing the door open quietly, found the nurse engaged in cooking a meal.

'May I come in, nurse?'

'Yes, Mr Larch.'

'You seem to have taken charge of the house,' he said, admiring her quick, neat movements; she was as much at home as if the kitchen had been her own.

'We often find it necessary,' she smiled. 'Nurses have to be ready for most things. Do you prefer tea or coffee for breakfast?'

'Surely you aren't getting breakfast for me? I could have had something in town.'

'Surely I am,' she said. 'If you aren't fastidious, I'll make tea. Miss Aked has had a moderately good night . . . I've told her . . . She took it very well, said she expected it. Of course there's a lot to be done, but I can't bother her yet. We ought to have a telegram from Mrs Hopkins, her aunt, this morning.'

'I wish you would give Miss Aked a message from me,' Richard broke in. 'Tell her I shall be very glad to see after things – the funeral, you know, and so on – if she cares. I can easily arrange to take a holiday from the office.'

'I am sure that would relieve her from a lot of anxiety,' the nurse said appreciatively. To hide a certain confusion Richard suggested that he should be allowed to lay the cloth in the sitting-room, and she told him he would find it in a drawer in the sideboard. He wandered off, speculating upon Adeline's probable answer to his proposal. Soon he heard the rattling of cups and saucers, and the nurse's footstep on the stair. He laid the cloth, putting the cruet in the middle and the salt-cellars at opposite corners, and then sat down in front of the case of French books to scan their titles, but he saw nothing save a blur of yellow. After a long time the nurse came down again.

'Miss Aked says she cannot thank you enough. She will leave everything to you, – everything. She is very much obliged indeed. She doesn't think Mrs Hopkins will be able to travel, because of her rheumatism, and there is no one else. Here is the key of Mr Aked's desk, and some other keys – there should be about £20 in gold in the cash box, and perhaps some notes.'

He took the keys, feeling profoundly happy. 'I shall just go up to the office first,' he decided, 'and arrange to get off, and then come down here again. I suppose you will stay on till Miss Aked is better?'

'Oh, of course.'

'She will be in bed several days yet?'

'Probably. She might be able to sit up an hour or two the day after to-morrow – in her own room.'

'It wouldn't do for me to see her?'

'I think not. She is very weak. No, you must act on your own responsibility.'

He and the nurse had breakfast together, talking with the freedom of old friends. He told her all he knew of the Akeds, not forgetting to mention that Mr Aked and himself were to have collaborated in a book. When Richard let this out, she showed none of those signs of timid reverence which the laity are wont to exhibit in the presence of literary people.

'Indeed!' she said politely, and then after a little pause: 'I actually write verses myself sometimes.'

'You do? And are they published?'

'Oh, yes, but perhaps not on their merits. You see, my father has influence ——'

'A journalist, is he, perhaps?'

She laughed at the idea, and mentioned the name of a well-known novelist.

'And you prefer nursing to writing!' Richard ejaculated when he had recovered from the announcement.

'To anything in the world. That is why I am a nurse. Why should I depend on my father, or my father's reputation?'

'I admire you for not doing so,' Richard replied. Hitherto he had only read about such women, and had questioned if they really existed. He grew humble before her, recognising a stronger spirit. Yet her self-reliance somehow chafed him, and he directed his thoughts to Adeline's feminine trustfulness with a slight sense of relief.

The funeral took place on Sunday. Richard found the formalities to be fewer and simpler than he had expected, and no difficulties arose of any kind. Mrs Hopkins, as Adeline had forseen, was unable to come, but she sent a long letter full of advice, and offering her niece a temporary home. Adeline had not yet been allowed to leave her bed, but on the Sunday morning the nurse had said that she might sit up for an hour or two in the afternoon, and would like to see Richard then.

He returned to Carteret Street on foot when the funeral was over.

'You are glad it is all finished?' the nurse said.

'Yes,' he answered wearily. His mind had dwelt on Mr Aked that day, and the lonely futility of the man's life had touched him with chill, depressing effect. Moreover, now it came to the point, he rather dreaded than desired that first interview with Adeline after her uncle's death. He feared that despite any service he had rendered, they were not much more than acquaintances. He morbidly conjectured what she would say to him and how he would reply. But he was glad when the nurse left him alone at the door of Adeline's room. He knocked rather louder than he had intended, and after hesitating a second walked in. Adeline was seated in an armchair near the window, fully dressed in black, with a shawl over her shoulders. Her back was towards him, but he could see that she was writing a letter on her knee. She looked round suddenly as the door opened, and gave a little 'Oh!' at the same time lifting her hands. Her face was pale, her hair flat, and her eyes large and glittering. He went up to her.

'Mr Larch!' She held his hand in her thin white one with a soft, weak pressure, silently gazing at him while tears gathered in her upturned eyes. Richard trembled in every part of his body; he could not speak, and wondered what was the matter with him.

'Mr Larch, you have been very kind. I shall never be able to thank you.'

'I hope you won't bother about any thanks,' he said. 'Are you better?'
And yet he wished her to say more.

With apparent reluctance she loosed his hand, and he sat down near
her.

'What should I have done without you! . . . Tell me about to-day. You
can't think how relieved I am now that it is over – the funeral, I mean.'

He said there was nothing to tell.

'Were there many other funerals?'

'Yes, a lot.'

He answered her questions one after another; she seemed to be
interested in the least detail, but neither of them mentioned the dead
man. Her eyes seldom left him. When he suggested that she must dismiss
him as soon as she felt tired, she laughed, and replied that she was not
likely to be tired for a very long while, and that he must have tea with
her and nurse.

'I was writing to my two uncles in San Francisco when you came in,'
she said. 'They will be terribly upset about me at first, poor fellows, but I
have told them how kind you have been, and Uncle Mark always used to
say I had plenty of sense, so that ought to ease their minds.' She smiled.

'Of course you have made no definite plans yet?' he asked.

'No, I shan't settle anything at present. I want to consult you about
several things, but some other time, when I am better. I shall have
enough money, I think – that is one solid comfort. My aunt Grace – Mrs
Hopkins – has asked me to go and stay with her. Somehow I don't want
to go – you'll think it queer of me, I daresay, but I would really prefer to
stop in London.'

He noticed that she said nothing as to joining her uncles in San
Francisco.

'I fancy I shall like London,' she went on, 'when I know it.'

'You aren't thinking, then, of going to San Francisco?'

He waited apprehensively for her answer. She hesitated. 'It is so far – I
don't quite know how my uncles are situated –'

Evidently, for some reason, she had no desire to leave London
immediately. He was very content, having feared that she might pass at
once away from him.

They had tea on a little round chess-table. The cramped space and the
consequent necessity of putting spare plates of cake on the bed caused
some amusement, but in the presence of the strong, brusque nurse
Adeline seemed to withdraw within herself, and the conversation, such as
it was, depended on the other two.

'I have been telling Miss Aked,' the nurse said after tea was over, 'that
she must go to the seaside for a week or two. It will do her an immense
deal of good. What she needs most of all is change. I suggested

Littlehampton; it is rather a quiet spot, not too quiet; there is nice river scenery, and a quaint old port, and quantities of lovely rustic villages in the neighbourhood.'

'It would certainly be a good thing,' Richard agreed; but Adeline said, rather petulantly, that she did not wish to travel, and the project was not discussed further.

He left soon afterwards. The walk home seemed surprisingly short, and when he got to Raphael Street he could remember nothing of the thoroughfares through which he had passed. Vague, delicious fancies flitted through his head, like fine lines half recalled from a great poem. In his room there was a smell from the lamp, and the windows were shut tight.

'Poor old landlady,' he murmured benignantly, 'when will she learn to leave the windows open and not to turn down the lamp?'

Having unfastened one of the windows, he extinguished the lamp and went out on to the little balcony. It was a warm evening, with a cloudy sky and a gentle, tepid breeze. The noise of omnibuses and cabs came even and regular from Brompton Road, and occasionally a hansom passed up Raphael Street. He stood leaning on the front of the balcony till the stir of traffic had declined to an infrequent rumble, his thoughts a smiling, whirling medley impossible to analyse or describe. At last he came in, and, leaving the window ajar, undressed slowly without a light, and lay down. He had no desire to sleep, nor did he attempt to do so; not for a ransom would he have parted with the fine, full consciousness of life which thrilled through every portion of his being. The brief summer night came to an end; and just as the sun was rising he dozed a little, and then got up without a trace of fatigue. He went to the balcony again, and drank in all the sweet invigorating freshness of the morning. The sunlit streets were enveloped in an enchanted silence.

XVIII

Nearly three weeks later came the following letter from Adeline. In the meanwhile she had had a rather serious relapse, and he had seen her only once or twice for a few minutes.

My dear Mr Larch, – This time I am *quite* sure I am well again. Nurse is obliged to leave to-day, as she is wanted at a hospital, and she has persuaded me to go to Littlehampton *at once*, and given me the address of some rooms. I shall leave Victoria to-morrow (Wednesday) by the 1.10 train; Lottie will go with me, and the house will be locked up. Good-bye for the present, if I don't see you. We shall not stay more than a week or ten days. I will write to you from Littlehampton.

Ever yours most gratefully,

A.A.

P.S. I was expecting you down to-night.

"'If I don't see you"!' he repeated to himself, smiling, and examining Adeline's caligraphy, which he had not seen before. It was a bold but not distinguished hand. He read the note several times, then folded it carefully and put it in his pocket-book.

By reason of an unexpected delay at the office he almost missed her at Victoria. The train was due out at least a minute before he rushed into the station; fortunately trains are not invariably prompt. Adeline was leaning from a carriage window to hand a penny to a newspaper boy; the boy dropped the penny, and she laughed. She wore a black hat with a veil. Her cheeks were a little fuller, and her eyes less unnaturally brilliant, at any rate under the veil; and Richard thought that he had never seen her look so pretty.

'There it is, silly boy, there!' she was saying as he came up.

'I thought I'd just see if you were all right,' he panted. 'I should have been here earlier, only I was detained.'

'How kind of you to take so much trouble!' she said, taking his hand, and fixing her eyes intently on his. The guard came along to fasten the doors.

'Luggage all in?' Richard asked.

'Yes, thanks. Lottie saw to it while I got the tickets. I find she is quite an experienced traveller.' At which Lottie, effaced in a corner, blushed.

'Well, I hope you will enjoy yourself.' The whistle sounded, and the train jerked forward. Adeline began to wave a good-bye.

'I see there's a Sunday league trip to Littlehampton on Sunday,' he said, walking along with the train.

'Oh! Do come down.'

'You'd like me to?'

'Very much.'

'I will, then. Send me the address.'

She gave a succession of little nods, as the train carried her away.

XIX

Richard's eye travelled expectantly over the tanned crowd of men in flannels and gaily attired girls which lined the platform of Littlehampton station, but Adeline was not to be seen. He felt somewhat disappointed, and then decided that he liked her the better for not having come to meet him. 'Besides,' he thought, 'the train being a special is not in the time-table, and she would not know when it was due.'

Her lodging was in a long, monotonous terrace which ran at right angles to the seashore, turning its back upon the river. Noon was at hand, and the fierce rays of the unclouded sun were untempered by any breeze. The street lay hushed, for everyone was either at church or on the sands. In response to his inquiry, the landlady said that Miss Aked was out, and had left a message that if a gentleman called, he was to follow her to the jetty. Obeying the directions given to him, Richard soon found himself by the banks of the swift little Arun, with the jetty some distance in front, and beyond that the sea, which shimmered blindingly in the heat. Throngs of respectably dressed people wandered up and down, and a low, languid murmur of conversation floated out as it were from the cavities of a thousand parasols. Perspiring children whose hands were chafed by gloves full of creases ran to and fro among the groups, shouting noisily, and heedless of the frequent injunction to remember what day it was. Here and there nurses pushing perambulators made cool spots of whiteness in the confusion of colour. On the river boats and small yachts were continually sweeping towards the sea on the ebbing tide; now and then a crew of boys would attempt to pull a skiff against the rapid current, persevere for a few strokes, and then, amid scoffs from the bank, ignominiously allow themselves to be whirled past the jetty with the other craft.

Richard had never seen a southern watering-place before, and he had fondly expected something different from Llandudno, Rhyl, or Blackpool, something less stolid and more continental. Littlehampton fell short of his anticipations. It was unpicturesque as a manufacturing town, and its summer visitors were an infestive, lower-middle class folk, garishly clothed, and unlearned in the fine art of enjoyment. The pure accent of London sounded on every side from the lips of clerks and shop-girls and their kin. Richard forgot that he was himself a clerk, looking not out of place in that scene.

Presently he espied a woman who seemed to belong to another sphere. She was leaning over the parapet of the jetty, and though a black and white sunshade entirely hid her head and shoulders, the simple, perfectly hung black skirt, the neatly shod foot, the small, smoothly gloved hand with thin gold circlet at wrist, sufficed to convince him that here, by some strange chance, was one of those exquisite creatures who on Saturday afternoons drove past the end of Raphael Street on their way to Hurlingham or Barnes. He wondered what she did there, and tried to determine the subtleties of demeanour and costume which constituted the plain difference between herself and the other girls on the jetty. At that moment she stood erect, and turned round. Why, she was quite young . . . He approached her . . . It was Adeline.

Astonishment was so clearly written on his face that she laughed as they exchanged greetings.

'You seem startled at the change in me,' she said abruptly. 'Do you know that I positively adore clothes, though I've only just found it out. The first thing I did when I got here was to go over to Brighton, and spend terrific sums at a dressmaker's. You see, there wasn't time in London. You don't despise me for it, I hope? I've plenty of money – enough to last a long, long time.'

She was dazzling, and she openly rejoiced in the effect her appearance had made on Richard.

'You couldn't have done better,' he answered, suddenly discovering with chagrin that his own serge suit was worn and shabby.

'I'm relieved,' she said; 'I was afraid my friend might think me vain and extravagant.' Her manner of saying 'my friend' – half mockery, half deference – gave Richard intense satisfaction.

They walked to the end of the jetty and sat down on a stone seat.

'Isn't it beautiful?' she exclaimed enthusiastically.

'What – the town, or the people, or the sea?'

'Everything. I've scarcely been to the sea-side before in all my life, and I think it's lovely.'

'The sea would be splendid if one could see it, but it blinds one even to glance at it in this heat.'

'You shall have half my sunshade.' She put it over him with a protective gesture.

'No, no,' he demurred.

'I say yes. Why don't men carry sunshades? It's only their pride that stops them . . . So you don't like the town and the people?'

'Well——'

'I love to see plenty of people about. And you would too, if you'd been fixed like me. I've never seen a real crowd. There are crushes when you go into theatres sometimes, aren't there?'

'Yes. Women faint.'

'But I shouldn't. I would have given anything not long ago to be in one of those crushes. Now, of course, I can just please myself. When we are back in London, do you think I could persuade you to take me?'

'You might,' he said, 'if you asked nicely. But young ladies who wear clothes like yours don't usually patronise the pit, where the crushes are. Stalls or dress circle would be more in your style. I propose we take the dress circle. You wouldn't enjoy your crush going in, but at the Lyceum and some other theatres, there is quite a superior crush coming out of the stalls and dress circle.'

'Yes, that is better. And I shall buy more clothes. Oh! I will be shockingly wasteful. If poor old uncle knew how his money was to be spent – '

A little child, chased by one still less, fell down flat in front of them, and began to cry. Adeline picked it up, losing her sunshade, and kissed both children. Then she took a paper of chocolates from her pocket and gave several to each child, and they ran away without saying thank you.

'Have one?' She offered the bag to Richard. 'That's another luxury I shall indulge in – chocolates. Do have just one, to keep me company,' she appealed. 'By the way, about dinner. I ordered dinner for both of us at my rooms, but we can improve on that. I have discovered a lovely little village a few miles away, Angmering, all old cottages and no drains. Let us drive there in a victoria, and picnic at a cottage. I know the exact place for us. There will be no people there to annoy you.'

'But you like "people," so that won't do at all.'

'I will do without "people" for this day.'

'And what shall we have for dinner?'

'Oh! Eggs and bread and butter and tea.'

'Tea, for dinner! Not very solid, is it?'

'Greedy! If you have such a large appetite, eat a few more chocolates; they will take it away.'

She rose, pointing to a victoria in the distance.

He looked at her without getting up, and their eyes met with smiles. Then he, too, rose. He thought he had never felt so happy. An intoxicating vision of future felicities momentarily suggested itself, only to fade before the actuality of the present.

The victoria stopped at Adeline's rooms. She called through the open window to Lottie, who came out and received orders to dine alone, or with the landlady if she preferred.

'Lottie and Mrs Bishop are great friends,' Adeline said. 'The silly girl would sooner stay in to help Mrs Bishop with housework than go out on the beach with me.'

'She must indeed be silly. I know which I should choose!' It seemed a remark of unutterable clumsiness – after he had said it, but Adeline's faint smile showed no dissatisfaction. He reflected that he would have been better pleased had she totally ignored it.

The carriage ran smoothly along the dusty roads, now passing under trees, and now skirting poppy-clad fields whose vivid scarlet almost encroached on the highway itself. Richard lay back, as he had seen men do in the Park, his shoulder lightly touching Adeline's. She talked incessantly, though slowly, in that low voice of hers, and her tones mingled with the measured trot of the enfeebled horse, and lulled Richard to a sensuous quiescence. He slightly turned his face towards

hers, and with dreamy deliberateness examined her features, – the dimple
in her cheek which he had never noticed before, the curves of her ear,
her teeth, her smooth black hair, the play of light in her eye; then his
gaze moved to her large felt hat, set bewitchingly aslant on the small
head, and then for a space he would look at the yellowish-green back of
the imperturbable driver, who drove on and on, little witting what
enchantment was behind him.

They consumed the eggs and bread and butter and tea which Adeline
had promised; and they filled their pockets with fruit. That was Adeline's
idea. She gave herself up to enjoyment like a child. When the sun was
less strenuous they walked about the village, sitting down frequently to
admire its continual picturesqueness. Time sped with astonishing rapidity;
Richard's train went at twenty-five minutes past seven, and already, as
they stood by the margin of the tiny tributary of the Arun, some
grandfather's clock in a neighbouring cottage clattered five. He was
tempted to say nothing about the train, quietly allow himself to miss it,
and go up by the first ordinary on Monday morning. But soon Adeline
inquired about his return, and they set off to walk back to Littlehampton;
the carriage had been dismissed. He invented pretexts for loitering, made
her sit on walls to eat apples, tried to get lost in by-paths, protested that
he could not keep the pace she set; but to no purpose. They arrived at
the station at exactly a quarter past seven. The platform was busy, and
they strolled to the far end of it and stood by the engine.

'I wish to heaven the train didn't leave so early,' he said. 'I'm sure the
sea air would do me a lot of good, if I could get enough of it. What a
beautiful day it has been!' He sighed sentimentally.

'I never, never enjoyed myself so perfectly,' she said emphatically.
'Suppose we beseech the engine-driver to lie still for a couple of hours?'
Richard's smile was inattentive.

'You are sure you haven't done too much?' he said with sudden
solicitude, looking at her half anxiously.

'I! not a bit. I am absolutely well again.' Her eyes found his and held
them, and it seemed to him that mystic messages passed to and fro.

'How long do you think of staying?'

'Not long. It gets rather boring, being alone. I expect I shall return on
Saturday.'

'I was thinking I would run down again on Saturday for the week-end –
take a week-end ticket,' he said; 'but of course, if——'

'In that case I should stay a few days longer. I couldn't allow myself to
deprive you of the sea air which is doing you so much good. By next
Saturday I may have discovered more nice places to visit, perhaps even
prettier than Angmering . . . But you must get in.'

He would have given a great deal just then to be able to say firmly: 'I have changed my mind about going. I will stay at a hotel tonight and take the first train tomorrow.' But it required more decision than he possessed, and in a few moments he was waving good-bye to her from the carriage window.

There were several other people in the compartment – a shy shop-girl and her middle-aged lover, evidently employees of the same establishment, and an artisan with his wife and a young child. Richard observed them intently, and found a curious, new pleasure in all their unstudied gestures and in everything they said. But chiefly he kept a watch on the shop-girl's lover, who made it no secret that he was dwelling in the seventh heaven. Richard sympathised with that man. His glance fell on him softly, benignantly. As the train passed station after station, he wondered what Adeline was doing, now, and now, and now.

On the following Saturday he took tea with Adeline at her lodgings. The train had been late, and by the time they were ready for the evening walk without which no visitor to the seaside calls the day complete, it was close upon nine o'clock. The beach was like a fair or a north-country wake. Conjurers, fire-eaters, and minstrels each drew an audience; but the principal attraction was a man and woman who wore masks and were commonly supposed to be distinguished persons to whom fate had been unkind. They had a piano in a donkey-cart, and the woman sang to the man's accompaniment. Just as Richard and Adeline came up, 'The River of Years' was announced for performance.

'Let us listen to this,' said Adeline.

They stood at the rim of the crowd. The woman had a rich contralto voice and sang with feeling, and her listeners were generous of both applause and coppers.

'I wonder who she is,' Adeline murmured, with a touch of melancholy, – 'I wonder who she is. I love that song.'

'Oh, probably some broken-down concert-singer,' Richard said curtly, 'with a drunken husband.'

'But she sang beautifully. She made me feel – you know – funny . . . A lovely feeling, isn't it?' She looked up at him.

'Yes,' he said, smiling at her.

'You're laughing.'

'Indeed I'm not. I know what you mean perfectly well. Perhaps I had it just then, too – a little. But the song is a bit cheap.'

'*I* could listen to it every day, and never get tired of listening. Don't you think that if a song gives *anyone* that – feeling, there must be some good in it?'

'Of course it's far better than most; but——'

'But not equal to those classical songs you told me about – the first

time I saw you, wasn't it? Yes, Schubert: was that the name? I mean to
get those, and you must show me the best ones, and play the
accompaniments, and then I shall judge for myself.'

'I shall make an awful mess of the accompaniments; they're not
precisely easy, you know.'

'Full of accidentals, are they? I sha'n't like them, then. I never do like
that sort of song.'

'But you will; you must.'

'Must I?' she almost whispered, in tones of gentle, feminine surrender.
And after a second or two: 'Then I'll try, if it will keep you in a good
temper.'

They stood fronting the sea. She looked straight ahead into the
darkening distance, and then turned round to him with a mock plaintive
expression, and they both laughed.

'Wouldn't it be better up by the river,' he suggested, 'where there are
fewer people?'

A little to his surprise, she agreed that it was certainly rather noisy and
crowded on the beach on Saturday nights, and they turned their backs to
the shore. The moon had risen, and shone at intervals through clouds.
For a few score yards they walked in silence. Then Adeline said, –

'It's very dull here during the week for a poor single woman like me. I
shall go home on Monday.'

'But think of London in this weather.'

'I do think of it. I think of the parks and the restaurants and the
theatres.'

'The good theatres are closed now.'

'Well, the music-halls. I've never been in one, and if they are very
naughty, then I want to go very much. Besides, there are lots of theatres
open. I've read all the theatrical advertisements in the "Telegraph," and
there must be plenty of things to see. You mayn't think them worth
seeing, but I should enjoy any theatre.'

'I believe you would,' he said. 'I used to be like that.'

'Up to now I've had no real pleasure – what I call pleasure – and I'm
just going to have it. I'll settle down afterwards.'

'Didn't your uncle take you out much?'

'I should say he didn't. He took me to a concert once. That was all –
in nearly two years. I suppose it never occurred to him that I was leading
a dull life.'

She made a movement with her hands, as if to put away from her all
the drab dailiness of her existence in Carteret Street.

'You can soon recover lost time,' Richard said cheerfully.

His fancy was in the rosy future, vividly picturing the light-hearted
gaieties, Bohemian, unconventional, artistic, in which he and she should

unite. He saw himself and Adeline becoming dearer to each other, and still dearer, her spirit unfolding like a flower, and disclosing new beauties day by day. He saw her eyes glisten when they met his; felt the soft pressure of her hand; heard her voice waver with tenderness, expectant of his avowal. And then came his own bold declaration: 'I love you, Adeline,' and her warm, willing lips were upon his. God! To dream of such beatitudes!

She had slightly quickened her step. The quays were silent and deserted, save for these two. Presently masts rose vaguely against the sky, and they approached a large ship. Richard leaned over the parapet to decipher the name on her bows. 'Juliane,' he spelt out.

'That is Norwegian or Danish.'

They lingered a few moments, watching the movements of dim figures on deck, listening to the musical chatter of an unknown tongue, and breathing that atmosphere of romance and adventure which foreign vessels carry with them from strange lands; then they walked on.

'Hush!' exclaimed Adeline, stopping, and touching Richard's arm.

The sailors were singing some quaint northern strain.

'What is it?' she asked when they had finished a verse.

'It must be a Norwegian folk-song. It reminds me of Grieg.'

Another verse was sung. It began to rain, – warm, summer drops.

'You will be wet,' Richard said.

'Never mind.'

A third verse followed, then a new air was started. It rained faster.

'Come under the shelter of the wall here,' Richard urged, timidly taking her arm. 'I think I see an archway.'

'Yes, yes,' she murmured, with sweet acquiescence; and they stood together a long time under the archway in silence, while the Norwegian sailors, heedless of weather, sang song after song.

The next morning the sky had cleared again, but there was a mist over the calm sea. They walked idly on the level sands. At first they were almost alone. The mist intensified distances; a group of little children paddling in a foot of water appeared to be miles away. Slowly the mist was scattered by the sun, and the beach became populous with visitors in Sunday attire. In the afternoon they drove to Angmering, Adeline having found no preferable haunt.

'You have no train to catch to-night,' she said; 'what a relief! Shall you start very early to-morrow?'

'I'm not particular,' he answered. 'Why?'

'I was thinking that Lottie and I would go up by the same train as you, but perhaps you won't care to be bothered with women and their luggage.'

'If you really intend to return to-morrow, I'll wire to Curpet not to expect me till after lunch, and we'll go at a reasonable hour.'

He left her at her lodging as the clock was striking eleven; but instead of making direct for his hotel, he turned aside to the river to have a last look at the 'Juliane.' Curiously, it began to rain, and he sheltered under the archway where he had stood with Adeline on the previous night. Aboard the 'Juliane' there was stir and bustle. He guessed that the ship was about to weigh anchor and drop down with the tide. Just after midnight she slid cautiously away from the quay, to the accompaniment of hoarse calls and the rattling of chains and blocks.

XX

During the journey to town Adeline would talk of nothing but her intention to taste all the amusements which London had to offer. She asked numberless questions with the persistency of an inquisitive child, while Lottie modestly hid herself behind a copy of 'Tit Bits,' which had been bought for her.

'Now I will read out the names of the plays advertised in the "Telegraph,"' she said, 'and you must tell me what each is like, and whether the actors are good, and the actresses pretty, and things of that kind.'

Richard entered with zest into the conversation. He was in a boisterous mood, and found her very willing to be diverted. Once, when he used a technical term, she stopped him: 'Remember, I have never been to a theatre.' On Sunday she had made the same remark several times. It seemed as if she liked to insist on the point.

The morning was delicious, full of light and freshness, and the torpid countryside through which the train swept at full speed suggested a gentle yet piquant contrast to the urban, gaslight themes which they were discussing. Though the sun shone with power, Adeline would not have the blinds drawn, but sometimes she used the newspaper for a shade, or bent her head so that the broad brim of her hat might come between her eyes and the sunshine. After an hour the talk slackened somewhat. As Richard, from his seat opposite, looked now at Adeline and now at the landscape, a perfect content stole over him. He wished that the distance to London could have been multiplied tenfold, and rejoiced in every delay. Then he began to miss the purport of her questions, and she had to repeat them. He was examining his heart. 'Is this love?' his thoughts ran. 'Do I actually love her now, – *now?*'

When the train stopped at New Cross, and Richard said that they would be at London Bridge in a few minutes, she asked when he would go down to Carteret Street.

'Any time,' he said.

'To-morrow night?'

He had hoped she would fix the same evening.

'When is the theatre-going to commence?' he queried.

She laughed vaguely: 'Soon.'

'Suppose I book seats for the Comedy?'

'We will talk about it to-morrow night.'

It appeared that her desire for the relaxations of town life had suddenly lost its instancy.

Immediately he reached the office he wrote a note to Mr Clayton Vernon. Some three hundred pounds was coming to him under the will of William Vernon, and he had purposed to let Mr Clayton Vernon invest this sum for him; but the letter asked that a cheque for £25 should be sent by return of post. Later in the afternoon he went to a tailor in Holborn, and ordered two suits of clothes.

He grew restless and introspective, vainly endeavouring to analyse his feeling towards Adeline. He wished that he had himself suggested that he should call on her that night, instead of allowing her to name Tuesday. When he got home, he looked at the letter which he had received from her a fortnight before, and then, enclosing it in a clean envelope, put it away carefully in his writing-case. He felt that he must preserve all her letters. The evening dragged itself out with desolating tedium. Once he went downstairs intending to go to the theatre, but returned before he had unlatched the front door.

Mrs Rowbotham laid his supper that evening, and he began to tell her about his holiday, mentioning, with fictitious *naïveté*, that he had spent it in the company of a young lady. Soon he gave the whole history of his acquaintance with the Akeds. She warmly praised his kindness towards Adeline.

'My Lily is keeping company with a young man,' she said, after a pause; 'a respectable young chap he is, a bus-conductor. This is his night off, and they're gone to the Promenade Concert. I didn't like her going at first, but, bless you, you have to give in. Young folk are young folk, all the world over . . . But I must be getting downstairs again. I have to do everything myself to-night. Ah! when a girl falls in love, she forgets her mother. It's natural, I suppose. Well, Mr Larch, it will be your turn soon, I hope.' With that she left the room quickly, missing Richard's hurried disclaimer.

'So you're engaged, Lily,' he said to the girl next morning.

Lily blushed and nodded; and as he looked at her eyes, he poignantly longed for the evening.

XXI

They sat by the window and talked till the day began to fade and the lamplighter had passed up the street. Several matters of business needed discussion, – the proving of Mr Aked's will, the tenancy of the house, and the opening of a new banking-account. Richard, who was acting informally as legal adviser, after the manner of solicitors' clerks towards their friends, brought from his pocket some papers for Adeline's signature. She took a pen immediately.

'Where do I put my name?'

'But you must read them first.'

'I shouldn't understand them a bit,' she said; 'and what is the use of employing a lawyer, if one is put to the trouble of reading everything one signs?'

'Well – please yourself. To-morrow you will have to go before a commissioner for oaths and swear that certain things are true; you'll be compelled to read the affidavits.'

'That I won't! I shall just swear.'

'But you simply must.'

'Sha'n't. If I swear to fibs, it will be your fault.'

'Suppose I read them out to you?'

'Yes, that would be nicer; but not now, after supper.'

For a few moments there was silence. She stood up and drew her finger in fanciful curves across the window-pane. Richard watched her, with a smile of luxurious content. It appeared to him that all her movements, every inflection of her voice, her least word, had the authenticity and the intrinsic grace of natural phenomena. If she turned her head or tapped her foot, the gesture was right, – having the propriety which springs from absolute self-unconsciousness. Her mere existence from one moment to the next seemed in some mysterious way to suggest a possible solution of the riddle of life. She illustrated nature. She was for him intimately a part of nature, the great Nature which hides itself from cities. To look at her afforded him a delight curiously similar to that which the townsman derives from a rural landscape. Her face had little conventional beauty; her conversation contained no hint either of intellectual powers or of a capacity for deep feeling. But in her case, according to his view, these things were unnecessary, would in fact have been superfluous. She *was*, and that sufficed.

Mingled with the pleasure which her nearness gave him, there were subordinate but distinct sensations. Except his sister Mary, he had never before been upon terms of close familiarity with any woman, and he realised with elation that now for the first time the latencies of manhood were aroused. His friendship – if indeed it were nothing else – with this gracious, inscrutable creature seemed a thing to be very proud of, to gloat upon in secret, to contemplate with a dark smile as one walked along the street or sat in a bus. . . . And then, with a shock of joyful, half-incredulous surprise, he made the discovery that she – she – had found some attractiveness in himself.

Their loneliness gave zest and piquancy to the situation. On neither side were there relatives or friends who might obtrude, or whom it would be proper to consult. They had only themselves to consider. Not a soul in London, with the exception of Lottie, knew of their intimacy, – the visit to Littlehampton, their plans for visiting the theatres, her touching reliance upon him. Ah, that confiding feminine trust! He read it frequently in her glance, and it gave him a sense of protective possession. He had approached no closer than to shake her hand, and yet, as he looked at the slight frame, the fragile fingers, the tufts of hair which escaped over her ears, – these things seemed to be his. Surely she had donned that beautiful dress for him; surely she moved gracefully for him, talked softly for him!

He left his chair, quietly lighted the candles at the piano, and began to turn over some songs.

'What are you doing?' she asked, from the window.

'I want you to sing.'

'Must I?'

'Certainly. Let me find something with an easy accompaniment.'

She came towards him, took up a song, opened it, and bade him look at it.

'Too difficult,' he said abruptly. 'Those arpeggios in the bass, – I couldn't possibly play them.'

She laid it aside obediently.

'Well, this?'

'Yes. Let us try that.'

She moved nearer to him, to miss the reflection of the candles on the paper, and put her hands behind her back. She cleared her throat. He knew she was nervous, but he had no such feeling himself.

'Ready?' he asked, glancing round and up into her face. She smiled timidly, flushing, and then nodded.

'No,' she exclaimed the next second, as he boldly struck the first chord. 'I don't think I'll sing. I can't.'

'Oh, yes, you will – yes, you will.'

'Very well.' She resigned herself.

The first few notes were tremulous, but quickly she gained courage. The song was a mediocre drawing-room ballad, and she did not sing with much expression, but to Richard's ear her weak contralto floated out above the accompaniment with a rich, passionate quality full of intimate meanings. When his own part of the performance was not too exacting, he watched from the corner of his eye the rise and fall of her breast, and thought of Keats's sonnet; and then he suddenly quaked in fear that all this happiness might crumble at the touch of some adverse fate.

'I suppose you call that a poor song,' she said when it was finished.

'I liked it very much.'

'You did? I am so fond of it, and I'm glad you like it. Shall we try another?' She offered the suggestion with a gentle diffidence which made Richard desire to abase himself before her, to ask what in the name of heaven she meant by looking to him as to an authority, a person whose will was to be consulted and whose humours were law.

Again she put her hands behind her back, cleared her throat, and began to sing. . . . He had glimpses of mystic, emotional deeps in her spirit hitherto unsuspected.

Lottie came in with a lamp.

'You would like supper?' Adeline said. 'Lottie, let us have supper at once.'

Richard remembered that when Mr Aked was alive, Adeline had been accustomed to go into the kitchen and attend to the meals herself; but evidently this arrangement was now altered. She extinguished the candles on the piano, and took the easy-chair with a question about Schubert. Supper was to be served without the aid of the mistress of the house. She had been training Lottie, – that was clear. He looked round. The furniture was unchanged, but everything had an unwonted air of comfort and neatness, and Adeline's beautiful dress scarcely seemed out of keeping with the general aspect of the room. He gathered that she had social aspirations. He had social aspirations himself. His fancy delighted to busy itself with fine clothes, fine furniture, fine food, and fine manners. That his own manners had remained inelegant was due to the fact that the tireless effort and vigilance which any amelioration of their original crudity would have necessitated, were beyond his tenacity of purpose.

The supper was trimly laid on a very white tablecloth, and chairs were drawn up. Lottie stood in the background for a few moments; Adeline called her for some trifling service, and then dismissed her.

'Won't you have some whisky? I know men always like a whisky at night.'

She touched a bell on the table.

'The whisky, Lottie – you forgot it.'

Richard was almost awed by her demeanour. Where could she have learnt it? He felt not unlike a bumpkin, and secretly determined to live up to the standard of deportment which she had set.

'You may smoke,' she said, when Lottie had cleared the table after supper; 'I like it. Here are some cigarettes – "Three Castles" – will they do?' Laughing, she produced a box from the sideboard, and handed it to him. He went to the sofa, and she stood with one elbow resting on the mantelpiece.

'About going to the theatre——' she began.

'May I take you? Let us go to the Comedy.'

'And you will book seats, the dress circle?'

'Yes. What night?'

'Let us say Friday. . . . And now you may read me those documents.'

When that business was transacted, Richard felt somehow that he must depart, and began to take his leave. Adeline stood erect, facing him in front of the mantelpiece.

'Next time you come, you will bring those Schubert songs, will you not?'

Then she rang the bell, shook hands, and sat down. He went out; Lottie was waiting in the passage with his hat and stick.

XXII

Seven or eight weeks passed.

During that time Richard spent many evenings with Adeline, at the theatre, at concerts, and at Carteret Street. When they were going up to town, he called for her in a hansom. She usually kept him waiting a few minutes. He sat in the sitting-room, listening to the rattle of harness and the occasional stamp of a hoof outside. At length he heard her light step on the stairs, and she entered the room, smiling proudly. She was wonderfully well dressed, with modish simplicity and exact finish, and she gave him her fan to hold while she buttoned her long gloves. Where she ordered her gowns he never had the least notion. They followed one another in rapid succession, and each seemed more beautiful than the last. All were sober in tint; the bodices were V-shaped, and cut rather low.

Lottie carefully placed a white wrap over her mistress's head, and then they were off. In the hansom there was but little conversation, and that of a trivial character. In vain he endeavoured to entice her into discussions. He mentioned books which he had read; she showed only a perfunctory interest. He explained why, in his opinion, a particular play was good and another bad; generally she preferred the wrong one, or at best maintained that she liked all plays, and therefore would not draw comparisons. Sometimes she would argue briefly about the conduct of certain characters in a piece, but he seldom found himself genuinely in agreement with her, though as a rule he verbally concurred. In music she was a little less unsympathetic towards his ideals. They had tried over several of his favourite classical songs, and he had seen in her face, as she listened, or hummed the air, a glow answering to his own enthusiasm. She had said that she would learn one of them, but the promise had not been kept, though he had reminded her of it several times.

These chagrins, however, were but infinitesimal ripples upon the smooth surface of his happiness. All of them together were as nothing compared to the sensations which he experienced in helping her out of the cab, in the full glare of a theatre façade. Invariably he overpaid the driver, handing him the silver with an inattentive gesture, while Adeline waited on the steps, – dainty food for the eyes of loiterers and passers-by. He offered his arm, and they passed down the vestibule and into the auditorium. With what artless enjoyment she settled herself in her seat, breathing the atmosphere of luxury and display as if it had been ozone, smiling radiantly at Richard, and then eagerly examining the occupants of the boxes through a small, silver-mounted glass! She was never moved by the events on the stage, and whether it happened to be tragedy or burlesque at which they were assisting, she turned to Richard at the end of every act with the same happy, contented smile, and usually began to make remarks upon the men and women around her. It was the playhouse and not the play of which she was really fond.

After the fall of the curtain, they lingered till most of the audience had gone. Sometimes they supped at a restaurant. 'It is my turn,' she would say now and then, when the obsequious waiter presented the bill, and would give Richard her purse. At first, for form's sake, he insisted on his right to pay, but she would not listen. He wondered where she had caught the pretty trick of handing over her purse instead of putting down the coins, and he traced it to a play which they had seen at the Vaudeville theatre. Yet she did it with such naturalness that it did not seem to have been copied. The purse was small, and always contained several pounds in gold, with a little silver. The bill paid, he gave it back to her with a bow.

Then came the long, rapid drive home, through interminable lamp-lined streets, peopled now only by hansoms and private carriages, past all the insolent and garish splendours of Piccadilly clubs, into whose unveiled windows Adeline eagerly gazed; past the mysterious, night-ridden Park; past the dim, solemn squares and crescents of Kensington and Chelsea, and so into the meaner vicinage of Fulham. It was during these midnight journeys, more than at any other time, that Richard felt himself to be a veritable inhabitant of the City of Pleasure. Adeline, flushed with the evening's enjoyment, talked of many things, in her low, even voice, which was never raised. Richard answered briefly; an occasional reply was all she seemed to expect.

Immediately, on getting out of the cab, she said good-night, and entered the house alone, while Richard directed the driver back to Raphael Street. Returning thus, solitary, he endeavoured to define what she was to him, and he to her. Often, when actually in her presence, he ventured to ask himself, 'Am I happy? Is this pleasure?' But as soon as he had left her, his doubtfulness vanished, and he began to long for their next meeting. Little phrases of hers, unimportant gestures, came back vividly to his memory; he thought how instinct with charm they were. And yet, was he really, truly in love? Was she in love? Had there been a growth of feeling since that night at Carteret Street after the holiday at Littlehampton? He uncomfortably suspected that their hearts had come nearer to each other that night than at any time since.

He tried to look forward to the moment when he should invite her to be his wife. But was that moment approaching? At the back of his mind lay an apprehension that it was not. She satisfied one part of his nature. She was the very spirit of grace; she was full of aplomb and a delicate tact; she had money. Moreover, her constant reliance upon him, her clinging womanishness, the caressing, humouring tone which her voice could assume, powerfully affected him. He divined darkly that he was clay in her hands; that all the future, even the future of his own heart, depended entirely upon her. If she chose, she might be his goddess. . . . And yet she had sharp limitations. . . .

Again, was she in love?

When he woke up of a morning he wondered how long his present happiness would continue, and whither it was leading him. A scrap of conversation which he had had with Adeline recurred to him frequently. He had asked her, once when she had complained of ennui, why she did not become acquainted with some of her neighbours.

'I don't care for my neighbours,' she replied curtly.

'But you can't live without acquaintances all your life.'

'No, not all my life,' she said with significant emphasis.

XXIII

They had been to the National Gallery; it was Saturday afternoon. Adeline said that she would go home; but Richard, not without a little trouble, persuaded her to dine in town first; he mentioned a French restaurant in Soho.

As they walked up Charing Cross Road, he pointed out the Crabtree, and referred to the fact that at one time he had frequented it reguarly. She stopped to look at its white-and-gold frontage. In enamel letters on the windows were the words: 'Table d'hôte, 6 to 9, 1/6.'

'Is it a good place?' she asked.

'The best in London – of that kind.'

'Then let us dine there; I have often wanted to try a vegetarian restaurant.'

Richard protested that she would not like it.

'How do you know? If you have been so often, why shouldn't I go once?' She smiled at him, and turned to cross the street; he hung back.

'But I only went for economy.'

'Then we will only go for economy to-day.'

He dangled before her the attractions of the French restaurant in Soho, but to no purpose. He was loth to visit the Crabtree. Most probably Miss Roberts would be on duty within, and he felt an inscrutable unwillingness to be seen by her with Adeline. . . . At last they entered. Looking through the glass doors which lead to the large, low-ceiled dining-room on the first floor, Richard saw that it was nearly empty, and that the cash-desk, where Miss Roberts was accustomed to sit, was for the moment unoccupied. He led the way in rather hurriedly, and selected places in a far corner. Although it was scarcely beginning to be dusk, the table electric lights were turned on, and their red shades made glimmering islands of radiance about the room.

Richard kept a furtive watch on the cash-desk; presently he saw Miss Roberts take her seat behind it, and shifted his glance to another quarter. He was preoccupied, and answered at random Adeline's amused queries as to the food. Between the soup and the entrée they were kept waiting; and Adeline, Richard being taciturn, moved her chair in order to look round the room. Her roving eyes stopped at the cash-desk, left it, and returned to it. Then a scornful smile, albeit scarcely perceptible, appeared on her face; but she said nothing. Richard saw her glance curiously at the cash-desk several times, and he knew, too, that Miss Roberts had discovered them. In vain he assured himself that Miss Roberts was not concerned in his affairs; he could not dismiss a sensation of uneasiness and discomfort. Once he fancied that the eyes of the two girls met, and that both turned away suddenly.

When the dinner was over, and they were drinking the coffee for which the Crabtree is famous, Adeline said abruptly, –

'I know someone here.'

'Oh!' said Richard, with fictitious nonchalance. 'Who?'

'The girl at the pay-desk, – Roberts, her name is.'

'Where have you met her?' he inquired.

Adeline laughed inimically. He was startled, almost shocked, by the harsh mien which transformed her face.

'You remember one night, just before uncle died,' she began, bending towards him, and talking very quietly. 'Someone called while you and I were in the sitting-room, to inquire how he was. That was Laura Roberts. She used to know uncle – she lives in our street. He made love to her – she didn't care for him, but he had money and she encouraged him. I don't know how far it went – I believe I stopped it. Oh! men are the strangest creatures. Fancy, she's not older than me, and uncle was over fifty!'

'Older than you, surely!' Richard put in.

'Well, not much. She knew I couldn't bear her, and she called that night simply to annoy me.'

'What makes you think that?'

'Think! I know it. . . . But you must have heard of the affair. Didn't they talk about it at your office?'

'I believe it was mentioned once,' he said hastily.

She leaned back in her chair, with the same hard smile. Richard felt sure that Miss Roberts had guessed they were talking about herself, and that her eyes were fixed on them, but he dared not look up for confirmation; Adeline gazed boldly around her. They were antagonistic, these two women, and Richard, do what he would, could not repress a certain sympathy with Miss Roberts. If she had encouraged Mr Aked's advances, what of that? It was no mortal sin, and he could not appreciate the reason of Adeline's strenuous contempt for her. He saw a little gulf widening between himself and Adeline.

'What tremendously red hair that girl has!' she said, later on.

'Yes, but doesn't it look fine!'

'Ye-es,' Adeline agreed condescendingly.

When he paid the bill, on the way out, Miss Roberts greeted him with an inclination of the head. He met her eye steadily, and tried not to blush. As she checked the bill with a tapping pencil, he could not help remarking her face. Amiability, candour, honesty, were clearly written on its attractive plainness. He did not believe that she had been guilty of running after Mr Aked for the sake of his money. The tales told by Jenkins were doubtless ingeniously exaggerated; and as for Adeline, Adeline was mistaken.

'Good evening,' Miss Roberts said simply, as they went out. He raised his hat.

'You know her, then!' Adeline exclaimed in the street.

'Well,' he answered, 'I've been going there, off and on, for a year or two, and one gets acquainted with the girls.' His tone was rather petulant. With a quick, winning smile, she changed the subject, and he suspected her of being artful.

XXIV

'I am going to America,' she said.

They sat in the sitting-room at Carteret Street. Richard had not seen her since the dinner at the vegetarian restaurant, and these were almost the first words she addressed to him. Her voice was as tranquil as usual; but he discerned, or thought he discerned, in her manner a consciousness that she was guilty towards him, that at least she was not treating him justly.

The blow was like that of a bullet: he did not immediately feel it.

'Really?' he questioned foolishly, and then, though he knew that she would never return: 'For how long are you going, and how soon?'

'Very soon, because I always do things in a hurry. I don't know for how long. It's indefinite. I have had a letter from my uncles in San Francisco, and they say I *must* join them; they can't do without me. They are making a lot of money now, and neither of them is married. . . . So I suppose I must obey like a good girl. You see I have no relatives here, except Aunt Grace.'

'You may never come back to England?'

(Did she colour, or was it Richard's fancy?)

'Well, I expect I may visit Europe sometimes. It wouldn't do to give England up entirely. There are so many nice things in England, – in London especially . . .'

Once, in late boyhood, he had sat for an examination which he felt confident of passing. When the announcement arrived that he had failed, he could not believe it, though all the time he knew it to be true. His thoughts ran monotonously: 'There must be some mistake; there must be some mistake!' and like a little child in the night, he resolutely shut his eyes to keep out the darkness of the future. The same puerility marked him now. Assuming that Adeline fulfilled her intention, his existence in London promised to be tragically cheerless. But this gave him no immediate concern, because he refused to contemplate the possibility of their intimacy being severed. He had, indeed, ceased to think; somewhere at the back of the brain his thoughts lay in wait for him. For the next two hours (until he left the house) he lived mechanically, as it were, and not by volition, subsisting merely on a previously acquired momentum.

He sat in front of her and listened. She began to talk of her uncles Mark and Luke. She described them in detail, told stories of her childhood, even recounted the common incidents of her daily life with them. She dwelt on their kindness of heart, and their affection for herself; and with it all she seemed a little to patronise them, as though she had been accustomed to regard them as her slaves.

'They are rather old-fashioned,' she said, 'unless they have altered. Since I heard from them, I have been wondering what they would think about my going to theatres and so on – with you.'

'What should they think?' Richard broke in. 'There's nothing whatever in that. London isn't a provincial town, or even an American city.'

'I shall tell them all about you,' she went on, 'and how kind you were to me when I scarcely knew you at all. You couldn't have been kinder if you'd been my only cousin.'

'Say "brother,"' he laughed awkwardly.

'No, really, I'm quite serious. I never thanked you properly. Perhaps I seemed to take it all as a matter of course.'

He wished to heaven she would stop.

'I'm disgusted that you are going,' he grumbled, putting his hands behind his head, – 'disgusted.'

'In many ways I am sorry too. But don't you think that I am doing the right thing?'

'How am I to tell?' he returned quickly. 'All I know is that when you go I shall be left all alone by my little self. You must think of me sometimes in my lonely garret.' His tone was light and whimsical, but she would not follow his lead.

'I shall often think of you,' she said musingly, scanning intently the toe of her shoe.

It seemed to him that she desired to say something serious, to justify herself to him, but could not gather courage to frame the words.

When he got out of the house, his thoughts sprang forth. It was a chilly night; he turned up the collar of his overcoat, plunged his hands deep into the pockets, and began to walk hurriedly, heedlessly, while examining his feelings with curious deliberation. In the first place, he was inexpressibly annoyed. 'Annoyed,' – that was the right word. He could not say that he loved her deeply, or that there was a prospect of his loving her deeply, but she had become a delightful factor in his life, and he had grown used to counting upon her for society. Might he not, in time, conceivably have asked her to marry him? Might she not conceivably have consented? In certain directions she had disappointed him; beyond doubt her spiritual narrowness had checked the growth of a passion which he had sedulously cherished and fostered in himself. Yet, in spite of that, her feminine grace, her feminine trustfulness, still exercised a strong and delicate charm. She was a woman and he was a man, and each was the only friend the other had; and now she was going away. The mere fact that she found a future with her uncles in America more attractive than the life she was then leading, cruelly wounded his self-love. He, then, was nothing to her, after all; he had made no impression;

she could relinquish him without regret! At that moment she seemed above and beyond him. He was the poor earthling; she the winged creature that soared in freedom now here, now there, giving her favours lightly, and as lightly withdrawing them.

One thing came out clear: he was an unlucky fellow.

He ran over in his mind the people who would remain to him in London when she had gone. Jenkins, Miss Roberts – Bah! how sickeningly commonplace were they! *She* was distinguished. She had an air, a *je ne sais quoi*, which he had never observed in a woman before. He recalled her gowns, her gestures, her turns of speech, – all the instinctive touches by which she proved her superiority.

It occurred to him fancifully that there was a connection between her apparently sudden resolve to leave England, and their visit to the Crabtree and encounter with Miss Roberts. He tried to see in that incident a premonition of misfortune. What morbid fatuity!

Before he went to sleep that night he resolved that at their next meeting he would lead the conversation to a frank discussion of their relations and 'have it out with her.' But when he called at Carteret Street two days later, he found it quite impossible to do any such thing. She was light-hearted and gay, and evidently looked forward to the change of life with pleasure. She named the day of departure, and mentioned that she had arranged to take Lottie with her. She consulted him about a compromise, already effected, with her landlord as to the remainder of the tenancy, and said she had sold the furniture as it stood, for a very small sum, to a dealer. It hurt him to think that she had given him no opportunity of actively assisting her in the hundred little matters of business involved in a change of hemisphere. What had become of her feminine reliance upon him?

He felt as if some object was rapidly approaching to collide with and crush him, and he was powerless to hinder it.

Three days, two days, one day more!

XXV

The special train for Southampton, drawn up against the main-line platform at Waterloo, seemed to have resigned itself with an almost animal passivity to the onslaught of the crowd of well-dressed men and women who were boarding it. From the engine a thin column of steam rose lazily to the angular roof, where a few sparrows fluttered with sudden swoops and short flights. The engine-driver leaned against the side of the cab, stroking his beard; the stoker was trimming coal on the tender. Those two knew the spectacle by heart: the scattered piles of steamer trunks amidst which passengers hurried hither and thither with no apparent object; the continual purposeless opening and shutting of carriage doors; the deferential gestures of the glittering guard as he bent an ear to ladies whose footmen stood respectfully behind them; the swift movements of the bookstall clerk selling papers, and the meditative look of the bookstall manager as he swept his hand along the shelf of new novels and selected a volume which he could thoroughly recommend to the customer in the fur coat; the long colloquies between husbands and wives, sons and mothers, daughters and fathers, fathers and sons, lovers and lovers, punctuated sometimes by the fluttering of a handkerchief, or the placing of a hand on a shoulder; the unconcealed agitation of most and the carefully studied calm of a few; the grimaces of porters when passengers had turned away; the slow absorption by *their* train of all the luggage and nearly all the people; the creeping of the clock towards the hour; the kisses; the tears; the lowering of the signal, – to them it was no more than a common street-scene.

Richard, having obtained leave from the office, arrived at a quarter to twelve. He peered up and down. Could it be that she was really going? Not even yet had he grown accustomed to the idea, and at times he still said to himself, 'It isn't really true; there must be some mistake.' The moment of separation, now that it was at hand, he accused of having approached sneakingly to take him unawares. He was conscious of no great emotion, such as his æsthetic sense of fitness might have led him to expect, – nothing but a dull joylessness, the drab, negative sensations of a convict foretasting a sentence of years.

There she stood, by the bookstall, engaged in lively talk with the clerk, while other customers waited. Lottie was beside her, holding a bag. The previous night they had slept at Morley's Hotel.

'Everything is all right, I hope?' he said, eyeing her narrowly, and feeling extremely sentimental.

'Yes, thank you. . . . Lottie, you must go and keep watch over our seats. . . . Well,' she went on briskly, when they were alone, 'I am actually going. I feel somehow as if it can't be true.'

'Why, that is exactly how I have felt for days!' he answered, allowing his voice to languish, and then fell into silence. He assiduously coaxed himself into a mood of resigned melancholy. With sidelong glances, as they walked quietly down the platform, he scanned her face, decided that it was divine, and dwelt lovingly on the thought: 'I shall never see it again.'

'A dull day for you to start!' he murmured, in tones of gentle concern.

'Yes, and do you know, a gentleman in the hotel told me we should be certain to have bad weather, and that made me so dreadfully afraid that I nearly resolved to stay in England.' She laughed.

'Ah, if you would!' he had half a mind to exclaim, but just then he became aware of his affectation and trampled on it. The conversation proceeded naturally to the subject of seasickness and the little joys and perils of the voyage. Strange topics for a man and a woman about to be separated, probably for ever! And yet Richard, for his part, could think of none more urgent.

'I had better get in now, had I not?' she said. The clock stood at five minutes to noon. Her face was sweetly serious as she raised it to his, holding out her hand.

'Take care of yourself,' was his fatuous parting admonition.

Her hand rested in his own, and he felt it tighten. Beneath the veil the colour deepened a little in her rosy cheeks.

'I didn't tell you,' she said abruptly, 'that my uncles had begged me to go to them weeks and weeks ago. I didn't tell you – and I put them off – because I thought I would wait and see if you and I – cared for each other.'

It had come, the explanation! He blushed red, and stuck to her hand. The atmosphere was suddenly electric. The station and the crowd were blotted out.

'You understand?' she questioned, smiling bravely.

'Yes.'

He was dimly conscious of having shaken hands with Lottie, of the banging of many doors, of Adeline's face framed in a receding window. Then the rails were visible beside the platform, and he had glimpses of people hurriedly getting out of a train at the platform opposite. In the distance a signal clattered to the horizontal. He turned round, and saw only porters, and a few forlorn friends of the voyagers; one woman was crying.

Instead of going home from the office, he rambled about the thoroughfares which converge at Piccadilly Circus, basking in the night-glare of the City of Pleasure. He had four pounds in his pocket. The streets were thronged with swiftly rolling vehicles. Restaurants and theatres and music halls, in evening array, offered their gorgeous enticements, and at last he entered the Café Royal, and, ordering an elaborate dinner, ate it slowly, with thoughtful enjoyment. When he had finished, he asked the waiter to bring a 'Figaro.' But there appeared to be nothing of interest in that day's 'Figaro,' and he laid it down. . . . The ship had sailed by this time. Had Adeline really made that confession to him just before the train started, or was it a fancy of his? There was something fine about her disconcerting frankness . . . fine, fine. . . . And the simplicity of it! He had let slip a treasure. Because she lacked artistic sympathies, he had despised her, or at best underestimated her. And once

– to think of it! – he had nearly loved her. . . . With what astonishing rapidity their intimacy had waxed, drooped, and come to sudden death! . . . Love, what *was* love? Perhaps he loved her now, after all . . .

'Waiter!' He beckoned with a quaint movement of his forefinger which brought a smile to the man's face, – a smile which Richard answered jovially.

'Sir?'

'A shilling cigar, please, and a coffee and cognac.'

At about nine o'clock he went out again into the chill air, and the cigar burnt brightly between his lips. He had unceremoniously dismissed the too importunate image of Adeline, and he was conscious of a certain devil-may-care elation.

Women were everywhere on the pavements. They lifted their silk skirts out of the mud, revealing ankles and lace petticoats. They smiled on him. They lured him in foreign tongues and in broken English. He broadly winked at some of the more youthful ones, and they followed him importunately, only to be shaken off with a laugh. As he walked, he whistled or sang all the time. He was cut adrift, he explained to himself, and through no fault of his own. His sole friend had left him (much she cared!), and there was none to whom he owed the slightest consideration. He was at liberty to do what he liked, without having to consider first, 'What would *she* think of this?' Moreover, he must discover solace, poor blighted creature! Looking down a side street, he saw a man talking to a woman. He went past them, and heard what they said. Then he was in Shaftesbury Avenue. Curious sensations fluttered through his frame. With an insignificant oath, he nerved himself to a resolve. Several times he was on the very point of carrying it out when his courage failed. He traversed the Circus, got as far as St James's Hall, and returned upon his steps. In a minute he was on the north side of Coventry Street. He looked into the faces of all the women, but in each he found something to repel, to fear.

Would it end in his going quietly home? He crossed over into the seclusion of Whitcomb Street to argue the matter. As he was passing the entry to a court, a woman came out, and both had to draw back to avoid a collision.

'*Chéri!*' she murmured. She was no longer young, but her broad, Flemish face showed kindliness and good humour in every feature of it, and her voice was soft. He did not answer, and she spoke to him again. His spine assumed the consistency of butter; a shuddering thrill ran through him. She put her arm gently into his, and pressed it. He had no resistance. . . .

XXVI

It was the morning of Boxing Day, frosty, with a sky of steel grey; the streets were resonant under the traffic.

Richard had long been anticipating the advent of the New Year, when new resolutions were to come into force. A phrase from a sermon heard at Bursley stuck in his memory: *Every day begins a new year.* But he could not summon the swift, courageous decision necessary to act upon that adage. For a whole year he had been slowly subsiding into a bog of lethargy, and to extricate himself would, he felt, need an amount of exertion which he could not put forth unless fortified by all the associations of the season for such feats, and by the knowledge that fellow-creatures were bracing themselves for a similar difficult wrench.

Now that he looked back upon them, the fourteen months which had elapsed since Adeline's departure seemed to have succeeded one another with marvellous rapidity. At first he had chafed under the loss of her, and then gradually and naturally he had grown used to her absence. She wrote to him, a rather long letter, full of details about the voyage and the train journey and her uncles' home; he had opened the envelope half expecting that the letter might affect him deeply; but it did not: it struck him as a distinctly mediocre communication. He sent a reply, and the correspondence ended. He did not love her, probably never had loved her. A little sentiment: that was all. The affair was quite over. If it had been perhaps unsatisfactory, the fault was not his. A man, he reflected, cannot by taking thought fall in love (and yet this was exactly what he had attempted to do!), and that in any case Adeline would not have suited him. Still, at moments when he recalled her face and gestures, her exquisite feminality, and especially her fine candour at their parting, he grew melancholy and luxuriously pitied himself.

At the commencement of the year which was now drawing to a close he had attacked the art of literature anew, and had compassed several articles; but as one by one they suffered rejection, his energy had dwindled, and in a short time he had again entirely ceased to write. Nor did he pursue any ordered course of study. He began upon a number of English classics, finishing few of them, and continued to consume French novels with eagerness. Sometimes the French work, by its neat, severe effectiveness, would stir in him a vague desire to do likewise, but no serious sustained effort was made.

In the spring, when loneliness is peculiarly wearisome, he had joined a literary and scientific institution, for young men only, upon whose premises it was forbidden either to drink intoxicants or to smoke tobacco. He paid a year's subscription, and in less than a fortnight loathed not only the institution but every separate member and official of it.

Then he thought of transplanting himself to the suburbs, but the trouble of moving the library of books which by this time he had accumulated deterred him, as well as a lazy aversion for the discomforts which a change would certainly involve.

And so he had sunk into a sort of coma. His chief task was to kill time. Eight hours were due to the office and eight to sleep, and eight others remained to be disposed of daily. In the morning he rose late, retarding his breakfast hour, diligently read the newspaper, and took the Park on the way to business. In the evening, as six o'clock approached, he no longer hurried his work in order to be ready to leave the office immediately the clock struck. On the contrary, he often stayed after hours when there was no necessity to stay, either leisurely examining his accounts, or gossiping with Jenkins or one of the older clerks. He watched the firm's welfare with a jealous eye, offered suggestions to Mr Curpet which not seldom were accepted, and grew to be regarded as exceptionally capable and trustworthy. He could divine now and then in the tone or the look of the principals (who were niggardly with praise) an implicit trust, mingled – at any rate, in the case of the senior partner – with a certain respect. He grew more sedate in manner, and to the office boys, over whom he had charge, he was even forbidding; they disliked him, finding him a martinet more strict and less suave than Mr Curpet himself. He kept them late at night sometimes without quite sufficient cause, and if they showed dissatisfaction, told them sententiously that boys who were so desperately anxious to do as little as they could would never get on in the world.

Upon leaving the office he would stroll slowly through Booksellers' Row and up the Strand, with the gait of a man whose time is entirely his own. Once or twice a week he dined at one of the foreign restaurants in Soho, prolonging the meal to an unconscionable length, and repairing afterwards to some lounge for a cigar and a liqueur. He paid particular attention to his dress, enjoying the sensation of wearing good clothes, and fell into a habit of comparing his personal appearance with that of the men whom he rubbed shoulders with in fashionable cafés and bars. His salary sufficed for these petty extravagances, since he was still living inexpensively in one room at Raphael Street; but besides what he earned, his resources included the sum received from the estate of William Vernon. Seventy pounds of this had melted in festivities with Adeline, two hundred pounds was lent upon mortgage under Mr Curpet's guidance, and the other fifty was kept in hand, being broken into as infrequent occasion demanded. The mortgage investment did much to heighten his status not only with the staff but with his principals.

Seated in a wine-room or lager-beer hall, meditatively sipping from glass or tankard, and savouring a fragrant cigar, he contrived to extract a certain pleasure from the contemplation of his equality with the men around him. Many of them, he guessed with satisfaction, were in a worse or a less secure position than his own. He studied faces and made a practice of entering into conversation with strangers, and these chance encounters almost invariably left him with the impression that he had met a mental inferior. Steeping himself, as it were, in all the frivolous, lusory activities of the West End, he began to acquire that indefinable, unmistakable air of *savoir-faire* characteristic of the prosperous clerk who spends his leisure in public places. People from the country frequently mistook him for the young man-about-town of the society papers, familiar with every form of metropolitan chicane, luxury, and vice.

After breakfast he went out into the Park with his skates. The Serpentine had been frozen hard for more than a week, and yesterday, a solitary unit in tens of thousands, he had celebrated Christmas on the ice, skating from noon till nearly midnight, with brief intervals for meals. The exercise and the fresh air had invigorated and enlivened him, and this morning, as he plunged once more into the loose throng of skaters, his spirits were buoyant. It had been his intention to pass yet another day on the Serpentine; but a sudden, surprising fancy entered his head, flitted away, and returned again and again with such increasing allurement that he fell in love with it: Why not commence to write now? Why, after all, leave the new beginning till the New Year? Was it true – what he had mournfully taken for granted for a month past, and so lately as an hour ago – that he lacked the moral strength to carry a good resolution into effect at any time he chose? . . . In a moment he had sworn to work four hours before he slept that night.

The decision reached, his humour became unequivocally gay. He shot forward with longer, bolder strokes, enjoying with a keener zest the swift motion and the strange black-and-white, sylvan-urban scene about him. He forgot the year of idleness which lay immediately behind him, forgot every previous failure, in the passionate exultation of his new resolve. He whistled. He sang. He attempted impossible figures, and only laughed when they ended in a fall. A woman, skating alone, stumbled to her knees; he glided towards her, lifted her lightly, raised his hat, and was gone before she could thank him: it was neatly done; he felt proud of himself. As the clock struck twelve he took off his skates, and walked in a quiet corner of the Park, deliberating intently upon the plot of a story, which fortunately had been in his mind for several months.

When he came in to dinner, he gave Lily five shillings for a Christmas box, almost without thinking, and though he had no previous intention of doing so; and inquired when she was to be married. He ordered tea for four o'clock, so that the evening might be long. In the afternoon he read and dozed. At a quarter to five the tea-things were cleared away, the lamp was burning brightly, the blinds drawn, and his writing-materials arranged on the table. He lit a pipe and sat down by the fire. At last, at last, the old, long-abandoned endeavours were about to be resumed!

The story which he was going to write was called 'Tiddy-fol-lol.' The leading character was an old smith, to be named Downs, employed in the forge of a large iron foundry at Bursley. Downs was a Primitive Methodist of the narrowest type, and when his daughter fell in love with and married a sceneshifter at the local theatre, she received for dowry a father's curse. Once, in the foundry, Downs in speaking of the matter had referred to his daughter as no better than a 'Tiddy-fol-lol,' and for years afterwards a favourite sport of the apprentice boys was to run after him, at a safe distance, calling 'Tiddy-fol-lol, Tiddy-fol-lol.' The daughter, completely estranged from her parent, died in giving birth to a son who grew up physically strong and healthy, but half an idiot. At the age of twelve, quite ignorant of his grandfather's identity, he was sent by his father to work at the foundry. The other lads saw a chance for fun. Pointing out Downs to him in the forge, they told him to go close to the man and say 'Tiddy-fol-lol.' 'What dost thee want?' Downs questioned gruffly, when the boy stood before him with a vacant grin on his face. 'Tiddy-fol-lol,' came the response, in the aggravating, uninflected tones peculiar to an imbecile. Downs raised his tremendous arm in a flash of anger, and felled the youngster with a blow on the side of the head. Then he bade him rise. But the child, caught just under the ear, had been struck dead. Downs was tried for manslaughter, pronounced insane, and subsequently released as a harmless lunatic. The Salvation Army took charge of him, and he lived by selling 'War-Cries' in the streets, still pursued by boys who shouted 'Tiddy-fol-lol.'

Properly elaborated, Richard opined, such a plot would make a powerful story. In his brain the thing was already complete. The one difficulty lay in the selection of a strong opening scene; that done, he was sure the incidents of the tale would fall naturally into place. He began to cogitate, but his thoughts went wool-gathering most pertinaciously, though time after time he compelled them to return to the subject in hand by force of knitted brows. He finished his pipe and recharged it. The fire burnt low, and he put on more coal. Still no suitable opening scene presented itself. His spirits slowly fell. What ailed him?

At length, an idea! He was not going to fail, after all. The story must of course begin with a quarrel between old Downs and his daughter. He drew up to the table, took a pen, and wrote the title; then a few sentences, hurriedly, and then a page. Then he read what was written, pronounced it unconvincing rubbish and tore it up. Words were untractable, and, besides, he could not *see* the scene. He left the table, and after studying a tale of de Maupassant's, started on a new sheet, carefully imitating the manner of that writer. But he could by no means satisfy himself. Mrs Rowbotham appeared with the supper-tray, and he laid his writing-materials on the bed. During supper he took up de Maupassant once more, and at ten o'clock made yet a third attempt, well knowing beforehand that it would not be successful. The plot tumbled entirely to pieces; the conclusion especially was undramatic; but how to alter it? . . .

He was disgusted with himself. He wondered what would happen to him if he lost his situation. Supposing that the firm of Curpet and Smythe failed! Smythe was a careless fellow, capable of ruining the business in a month if for any reason Curpet's restraining influence was withdrawn. These and similar morbid fancies assailed him, and he went to bed sick with misery, heartily wishing that he had been less precipitate in his attempt to be industrious. He had a superstition that if he had waited for the New Year, the adventure might have resulted more happily.

In the night he awoke, to lament upon his solitariness. Why had he no congenial friends? How could he set about obtaining sympathetic companionship? He needed, in particular, cultured feminine society. Given that, he could work; without it he should accomplish nothing. He reflected that in London there were probably thousands of 'nice girls,' pining for such men as he. What a ridiculous civilisation it was that prevented him from meeting them! When he saw a promising girl in a bus, why in the name of heaven should he not be at liberty to say to her, 'Look here, I can convince you that I mean well; let us make each other's acquaintance'? . . . But convention, convention! He felt himself to be imprisoned by a relentless, unscalable wall. . . . Then he dreamt that he was in a drawing-room full of young men and women, and that all were chattering vivaciously and cleverly. He himself stood with his back to the fire, and talked to a group of girls. They looked into his face, as Adeline used to look. They grasped his ideals and his aims without laborious explanations; half a word was sufficient to enlighten them; he saw the gleam of appreciative comprehension in their eyes long before his sentences were finished. . . .

XXVII

The next morning was bright with sunshine; the frost had broken, and the streets were beginning to be muddy. Richard went out, his mind empty, and dully dejected. At Sloane Street he mounted a bus, taking the one vacant front seat on the top. For a little while he stared absently at the handle of his stick. Presently a chance movement of the head made him aware that someone's eyes were upon him. He looked round. In the far corner of the seat opposite was Miss Roberts. She hesitated, flushing, and then bowed, and he responded. No further communications were possible just then (and for this, at the moment, he felt thankful), because they were separated by two young gentlemen wearing tweed caps, and collars which might have been clean once, who were arguing briskly over a copy of the 'Sportsman.'

For some strange reason of diffidence, Richard had not been to the Crabtree since his visit there with Adeline. He was sardonically in search of his motive for staying away when the young gentlemen with the 'Sportsman' left the bus. Miss Roberts grew rosy as he got up and offered her his hand, at the same time seating himself by her side. She wore a black jacket and skirt, well worn but in good preservation, a hat with red flowers, and grey woollen gloves; and any person of ordinary discernment would have guessed her occupation without a great deal of difficulty. During the last year she had become stouter, and her figure was now full rather than slender; her features, especially the nostrils, mouth, and chin, were somewhat heavy, but she had prettily shaped ears, and her eyes, of no definable tint, were soft and tender; her reddish-brown hair was as conspicuous and as splendid as ever, coiled with tight precision at the back of her head, and escaping here and there above her ears in tiny flying wisps. The expression of her face was mainly one of amiability, but passive, animal-like, inert; she seemed full of good-nature.

'We haven't seen you at the Crabtree, lately,' she said.

'You are still at the old place, then?'

'Oh, yes; and shall be, I expect. They've taken another floor now, and we're the biggest vegetarian restaurant in London.'

There was a note of timid agitation in her voice, and he noticed besides that her cheeks were red and her eyes shone. Could it be that this encounter had given her pleasure? The idea of such a possibility afforded him secret delight. . . . She, a breathing woman, glad to see him! He wondered what the other people on the bus were thinking of them, and especially what the driver thought; the driver had happened to catch sight of them when they were shaking hands, and as Richard examined the contour of the man's rubicund face, he fancied he saw there the glimmer of a smile. This was during a little pause in the conversation.

'And how have you spent Christmas?' It was Richard's question.

'At home,' she answered simply, 'with father and mother. My married sister and her husband came over for the day.'

'And I spent mine all alone,' he said ruefully. 'No friends, no pudding, no nothing.'

She looked at him compassionately.

'I suppose you live in rooms? It must be very lonely.'

'Oh!' he returned lightly, yet seizing with eager satisfaction the sympathy she offered, 'it's nothing when you're used to it. This makes my third Christmas in London, and none of them has been particularly uproarious. Fortunately there was the skating this year. I was on the Serpentine nearly all day.'

Then she asked him if skating was easy to learn, because she had been wanting to try for years, but had never had opportunity. He answered that it was quite easy, if one was not afraid.

'I'm going your way,' he said, as they both got off at Piccadilly Circus, and they walked along Coventry Street together. The talk flagged; to rouse it Richard questioned her about the routine of the restaurant, – a subject on which she spoke readily, and with a certain sense of humour. When they reached the Crabtree, –

'Why, it's been painted!' Richard exclaimed. 'It looks very swagger, indeed, now.'

'Yes, my! doesn't it? And it's beautiful inside, too. You must come in sometime.'

'I will,' he said with emphasis.

She shook his hand quite vigorously, and their eyes met with a curious questioning gaze. He smiled to himself as he walked down Chandos Street; his dejection had mysteriously vanished, and he even experienced a certain uplifting of spirit. It occurred to him that he had never at all understood Miss Roberts before. How different she was outside the restaurant! Should he go to the Crabtree for lunch that day, or should he allow a day or two to elapse? He decided prudently to wait.

He debated whether he should mention the meeting to Jenkins, and said that on the whole he would not do so. But he found Jenkins surprisingly urbane, and without conscious volition he was soon saying, –

'Guess who I came down with on the bus this morning.'

Jenkins gave it up.

'Laura Roberts,' and then, seeing no look of comprehension on Jenkins' face, 'You know, the cashier at the Crabtree.'

'Oh – *her!*'

The stress was a little irritating.

'*I* saw her about a fortnight ago,' Jenkins said.

'At the Crabtree?'

'Yes. Did she say anything to you about me?' The youth smiled.

'No. Why?'

'Nothing. We had a talk, and I mashed her a bit, – that's all.'

'Ah, my boy, you won't get far with her.'

'Oh, sha'n't I? I could tell you a thing or two *re* Laura Roberts, if I liked.'

Although Jenkins' remark was characteristic, and Richard knew well enough that there was nothing behind his words, yet his mind reverted instantly to the stories connecting Miss Roberts with Mr Aked.

'Don't gas,' he said curtly. 'She looks on you as a boy.'

'Man enough for any woman,' said Jenkins, twirling the rudiments of a moustache.

The discussion might have gone further, had it not been interrupted by Mr Smythe, who burst suddenly into the room, as his custom was.

'Larch, come with me into Mr Curpet's room.' His tone was brusque. He had none of Mr Curpet's natural politeness, though on rare occasions, of which the present was not one, he sought clumsily to imitate it. Richard felt a vague alarm.

With a muffler round his throat, Mr Curpet was seated before the fire, blowing his nose and breathing noisily. Mr Smythe went to the window, and played with the tassel of the blind cord.

'We are thinking of making some changes, Larch,' Mr Curpet began.

'Yes, sir.' His heart sank. Was he to be dismissed? The next sentence was reassuring.

'In future all costs will be drawn and settled in the office, instead of being sent out. Do you feel equal to taking charge of that department?'

Richard had many times helped in the preparation of bills of costs, and possessed a fair knowledge of this complicated and engaging subject. He answered very decidedly in the affirmative.

'What we propose,' Mr Smythe broke in, 'is that you should have an assistant, and that the two of you should attend to both the books and the costs.'

'Of course your salary will be increased,' Mr Curpet added.

'Let me see, what do you get now?' This from Mr Smythe, whose memory was imperfect.

'Three pounds ten, sir.'

'Suppose we say four pounds ten,' said Mr Smythe to Mr Curpet, and then turning to Larch: 'That's very good indeed, you know, young man; you wouldn't get that everywhere. By Jove, no, you wouldn't!' Richard was fully aware of the fact. He could scarcely credit his own luck. 'And we shall expect you to keep things up to the mark.'

Mr Curpet smiled kindly over his handkerchief, as if to intimate that Mr Smythe need not have insisted on that point.

'And you may have to stay late sometimes,' Mr Smythe went on.

'Yes, sir.'

When the interview was finished, he retraced his career at the office, marvelling that he should have done anything unusual enough to inspire his principals to such appreciation, and he soon made out that, compared with others of the staff, he had indeed been a model clerk. A delicious self-complacence enveloped him. Mr Smythe had had the air of conferring a favour; but Mr Curpet was at the head of affairs at No. 2 Serjeant's Court, and Mr Curpet's attitude had been decidedly flattering. At first he had a difficulty in grasping his good fortune, thought it too good to be true; but he ended by believing in himself very heartily. In the matter of salary, he stood now second only to Mr Alder, he a youth not three years out of the provinces. Three years ago an income of £234 per annum would have seemed almost fabulous. His notions as to what constituted opulence had changed since then, but nevertheless £234 was an excellent revenue, full of possibilities. A man could marry on that and live comfortably; many men ventured to marry on half as much. In clerkdom he had indubitably risen with ease to the upper ranks. There was good Northern stuff in Richard Larch, after all! As he walked home, his brain was busy with plans, beautiful plans for the New Year, – how he would save money, and how he would spend his nights in toil.

XXVIII

There happened to be a room to let on the same floor as Richard's own. The rent was only five shillings per week, and he arranged to take it and use it as a bedroom, transforming the other and larger room into a study. Mrs Rowbotham was asked to remove all her tables, chairs, carpets, pictures, ornaments, and accessories from both rooms, as he proposed to furnish them entirely anew at his own cost. This did not indicate that a sudden increase of revenue had, as once on a previous occasion, engendered in him a propensity to squander. On the contrary, his determination to live economically was well established, and he hoped to save a hundred pounds per annum with ease. But the influence of an æsthetic environment upon his literary work would, he argued, probably be valuable enough to justify the moderate expenditure involved, and so all the leisure of the last days of the year was given to the realisation of certain theories in regard to the furnishing of a study and a bedroom. Unfortunately the time at his disposal was very limited – was it not essential that the place should be set in order by the 31st December, that work might commence on the 1st January? – but he did not spare himself, and the result, when he contemplated it on New Year's Eve, filled him with pleasure and pride. He felt that he could write worthily in that study, with its four autotype reproductions of celebrated pictures on the self-coloured walls, its square of Indian carpet over Indian matting, its long, low bookshelves, its quaint table with the elm top, its plain rush-bottomed chairs, and its broad luxurious divan. He marvelled that he had contrived so long to exist in the room as it was before, and complacently attributed his ill-success as a writer to the lack of harmonious surroundings. By the last post arrived a New Year's card from Mrs Clayton Vernon. Twelve months ago she had sent a similar kind token of remembrance, and he had ignored it; in the summer she had written inviting him to spend a few days at Bursley, and he had somewhat too briefly asked to be excused. To-night, however, he went out, bought a New Year's card, and despatched it to her at once. He flowed over with benevolence, viewing the world through the rosy spectacles of high resolve. Mrs Clayton Vernon was an excellent woman, and he would prove to her and to Bursley that they had not estimated too highly the possibilities of Richard Larch. He was, in truth, prodigiously uplifted. The old sense of absolute power over himself for good or evil returned. A consciousness of exceptional ability possessed him. The future, splendid in dreams, was wholly his; and yet again – perhaps more thoroughly than ever before – the ineffectual past was effaced. To-morrow was the New Year, and to-morrow the new heaven and the new earth were to begin.

He had decided to write a novel. Having failed in short stories and in essays, it seemed to him likely that the novel, a form which he had not so far seriously attempted, might suit his idiosyncrasy better. He had once sketched out the plot of a short novel, a tale of adventure in modern London, and on examination this struck him as ingenious and promising. Moreover, it would appeal – like Stevenson's 'New Arabian Nights,' which in Richard's mind it distantly resembled – both to the general and to the literary public. He determined to write five hundred words of it a day, five days a week; at this rate of progress he calculated that the book would be finished in four months; allowing two months further for revision, it ought to be ready for a publisher at the end of June.

He drew his chair up to the blazing fire, and looked down the vista of those long, lamplit evenings during which the novel was to grow under his hands. How different he from the average clerk, who with similar opportunities was content to fritter away those hours which would lead himself, perhaps, to fame! He thought of Adeline, and smiled. What, after all, did such as he want with women? He was in a position to marry, and if he met a clever girl of sympathetic temperament, he emphatically would marry (it did not occur to him to add the clause, 'Provided she will have me'); but otherwise he would wait. He could afford to wait, – to wait till he had made a reputation, and half a score of women, elegant and refined, were only too willing to envelop him in an atmosphere of adoration.

It was part of his plan for economy to dine always at the Crabtree, where one shilling was the price of an elaborate repast, and he went there on New Year's Day. As he walked up Charing Cross Road, his thoughts turned naturally to Miss Roberts. Would she be as cordial as when he had met her on the omnibus, or would she wear the polite mask of the cashier, treating him merely as a frequenter of the establishment? She was engaged when he entered the dining-room, but she noticed him and nodded. He looked towards her several times during his meal, and once her eyes caught his and she smiled, not withdrawing them for a few moments; then she bent over her account book.

His fellow-diners seemed curiously to have degenerated, to have grown still narrower in their sympathies, still more careless in their eating, still more peculiar or shabbier in their dress. The young women of masculine aspect set their elbows on the table more uncompromisingly than ever, and the young men with soiled wristbands or no wristbands at all were more than ever tedious in their murmured conversations. It was, indeed, a bizarre company that surrounded him! Then he reflected that these people had not altered. The change was in himself. He had outgrown them; he surveyed them now as from a tower. He was a man with a future, using this restaurant because it suited him temporarily to do so, while they would use it till the end, never deviating, never leaving the rut.

'So you have come at last!' Miss Roberts said to him when he presented his check. 'I was beginning to think you had deserted us.'

'But it's barely a week since I saw you,' he protested. 'Let me wish you a happy New Year.'

'The same to you.' She flushed a little, and then: 'What do you think of our new decorations? Aren't they pretty?'

He praised them perfunctorily, even without glancing round. His eyes were on her face. He remembered the reiterated insinuations of Jenkins, and wondered whether they had any ground of fact.

'By the way, has Jenkins been here to-day?' he inquired, by way of introducing the name.

'Is that the young man who used to come with you sometimes? No.'

There was no trace of self-consciousness in her bearing, and Richard resolved to handle Jenkins with severity. Another customer approached the pay-desk.

'Well, good afternoon.' He lingered.

'Good afternoon.' Her gaze rested on him softly. 'I suppose you'll be here again *some* time.' She spoke low, so that the other customer should not hear.

'I'm coming every day now, I think,' he answered in the same tone, with a smothered laugh. 'Ta-ta.'

That night at half-past seven he began his novel. The opening chapter was introductory and the words came without much effort. This being only a draft, there was no need for polish; so that when a sentence refused to run smoothly at the first trial, he was content to make it grammatical and leave it. He seemed to have been working for hours when a desire took him to count up what was already written. Six hundred words! He sighed the sigh of satisfaction, and looked at his watch, to find that it was exactly half-past eight. The discovery somewhat damped his felicity. He began to doubt whether stuff composed at the rate of ten words a minute could have any real value. Pooh! Sometimes one wrote quickly, and sometimes slowly. The number of minutes occupied was no index of quality. Should he continue writing? Yes, he would. . . . No. . . . Why should he? He had performed the task self-allotted for the day, and more; and now he was entitled to rest. True, the actual time of labour had been very short; but then, another day the same amount of work might consume three or four hours. He put away his writing-things, and searched about for something to read, finally lighting on 'Paradise Lost.' But 'Paradise Lost' wanted actuality. He laid it aside. Was there any valid reason why he should not conclude the evening at the theatre? None. The frost had returned with power, and the reverberation of the streets sounded invitingly through his curtained windows. He went out, and walked briskly up Park Side. At Hyde Park Corner he jumped on an omnibus.

It was the first night of a new ballet at the Ottoman. 'Standing-room only,' said the man at the ticket-office. 'All right,' said Richard, and, entering, was greeted with soft music, which came to him like a fitful zephyr over a sea of heads.

XXIX

One Saturday afternoon towards the end of February, he suddenly decided to read through so much of the draft novel as was written; hitherto he had avoided any sort of revision. The resolve to accomplish five hundred words a day had been kept indifferently well, and the total stood at about fourteen thousand. As he wrote a very bold hand, the sheets covered made quite a respectable pile. The mere bulk of them cajoled him, in spite of certain misgivings, into an optimistic surmise as to their literary quality. Never before had he written so much upon one theme, and were the writing good or bad, he was, for a few moments, proud of his achievement. The mischief lay in the fact that week by week he had exercised less and still less care over the work. The phrase, 'Anything will do for a draft,' had come to be uttered with increasing frequency as an excuse for laxities of style and construction. 'I will make that right in the revision,' he had reassured himself, and had gone negligently forward, leaving innumerable crudities in the wake of his hurrying pen. During the last few days he had written scarcely anything, and perhaps it was a hope of stimulating a drooping inspiration by the complacent survey of work actually done that tempted him to this hazardous perusal.

He whistled as he took up the manuscript, as a boy whistles when going into a dark cellar. The first three pages were read punctiliously, every word of them, but soon he grew hasty, rushing to the next paragraph ere the previous one was grasped; then he began shamelessly to skip; and then he stopped, and his heart seemed to stop also. The lack of homogeneity, of sequence, of dramatic quality, of human interest; the loose syntax; and the unrelieved mediocrity of it all, horrified him. The thing was dry bones, a fiasco. The certainty that he had once more failed swept over him like a cold, green wave of the sea, and he had a physical feeling of sickness in the stomach. . . . It was with much ado that he refrained from putting the whole manuscript upon the fire, and crushing it venomously into the flames with a poker. Then he steadied himself. His self-confidence was going, almost gone; he must contrive to recover it, and he sought for a way. (Where were now the rash exultations of the New Year?) It was impossible that his work should be irredeemably bad. He remembered having read somewhere that the difference between a fine and a worthless novel was often a difference of elaboration simply. A conscientious re-writing, therefore, might probably bring about a surprising amelioration. He must immediately make the experiment. But he had long since solemnly vowed not to commence the second writing till the draft was done; the moral value of finishing even the draft had then seemed to him priceless. No matter! Under stress of grievous necessity, that oath must be forsworn. No other course could save him from collapse.

He went out into the streets. The weather, fine and bright, suggested the earliest infancy of spring, and Piccadilly was full of all classes and all ages of women. There were regiments of men, too, but the gay and endless stream of women obsessed him. He saw them sitting in hansoms and private carriages and on the tops of omnibuses, niched in high windows, shining in the obscurity of shops, treading the pavements with fairy step, either unattended or by the side of foolish, unappreciative males. Every man in London seemed to have the right to a share of some woman's companionship, except himself. As for those men who walked alone, they had sweethearts somewhere, or mothers and sisters, or they were married and even now on the way to wife and hearth. Only he was set apart.

A light descended upon him that afternoon. The average man and the average woman being constantly thrown into each other's society, custom has staled for them the exquisite privilege of such intercourse. The rustic cannot share the townsman's enthusiasm for rural scenery; he sees no matter for ecstasy in the view from his cottage door; and in the same way the average man and the average woman dine together, talk together, walk together, and know not how richly they are therein blessed. But with solitaries like Richard it is different. Debarred from fellowship with the opposite sex by circumstance and an innate diffidence which makes the control of circumstance impossible, their starved sensibilities acquire a certain morbid tenderness. (Doubtless the rustic discerns morbidity in the attitude of the townsman towards the view from his cottage door.) Richard grasped this. In a luminous moment of self-revelation, he was able to trace the growth of the malady. From its first vague and fugitive symptoms, it had so grown that now, on seeing an attractive woman, he could not be content to say, 'What an attractive woman!' and have done with it, but he must needs build a house, furnish a room in the house, light a fire in the room, place a low chair by the fire, put the woman in the chair, with a welcoming smile on her upturned lips – and imagine that she was his wife. And it was not only attractive women that laid the spell upon him. The sight of any living creature in petticoats was liable to set his hysterical fancy in motion. Every woman he met was Woman. . . . Of the millions of women in London, why was he not permitted to know a few? Why was he entirely cut off? There they were: their silk skirts brushed him as they passed; they thanked him for little services in public vehicles; they ministered to him in restaurants; they sang to him at concerts, danced for him at theatres; touched his existence at every side – and yet they were remoter than the stars, unattainable as the moon. . . . He rebelled. He sank to despair, and rose to frenzies of anger. Then he was a pathetic figure, and extended to himself his own pity, smiling sardonically at fate. Fate was the harder to bear because he was convinced that, at the heart of him, he was essentially a woman's man. None could enjoy the feminine atmosphere more keenly, more artistically than he. Other men, who had those delicious rights for which he longed in vain, assessed them meanly, or even scorned them. . . . He looked back with profound regret to his friendship with Adeline. He dreamt that she had returned, that he had fallen in love with her and married her, that her ambitions were leading him forward to success. Ah! Under the incentive of a woman's eyes, of what tremendous efforts is a clever man not capable, and deprived of it to what deeps of stagnation will he not descend! Then he awoke again to the fact that he knew no woman in London.

Yes, he knew one, and his thoughts began to play round her

caressingly, idealising and ennobling her. She only gave him his change daily at the Crabtree, but he knew her; there existed between them a kind of intimacy. She was a plain girl, possessing few attractions, except the supreme one of being a woman. She was below him in station; but had she not her refinements? Though she could not enter into his mental or emotional life, did she not exhale for him a certain gracious influence? His heart went forth to her. Her flirtations with Mr Aked, her alleged dalliance with Jenkins? Trifles, nothings! She had told him that she lived with her mother and father and a younger brother, and on more than one occasion she had mentioned the Wesleyan chapel; he had gathered that the whole family was religious. In theory he detested religious women, and yet – religion in a woman . . . what was it? He answered the question with a man's easy laugh. And if her temperament was somewhat lymphatic, he divined that, once roused, she was capable of the most passionate feeling. He had always had a predilection for the sleeping-volcano species of woman.

XXX

Richard was soon forced to the conclusion that the second writing of his novel was destined to be a failure. For a few days he stuck doggedly to the task, writing stuff which, as he wrote it, he knew would ultimately be condemned. Then one evening he stopped suddenly, in the middle of a word, bit the penholder for a moment, and threw it down with a 'Damn!' This sort of thing could not continue.

'Better come up and see my new arrangements at Raphael Street to-night,' he said to Jenkins the next day. He wanted a diversion.

'Any whisky going?'

'Certainly.'

'Delighted, I'm sure,' said Jenkins, with one of his ridiculous polite bows. He regarded these rare invitations as an honour; it was more than six months since the last.

They drank whisky and smoked cigars which Jenkins had thoughtfully brought with him, and chattered for a long time about office matters. And then, as the cigar-ash accumulated, the topics became more personal and intimate. That night Jenkins was certainly in a serious vein; further, he was on his best behaviour, striving to be sympathetic and gentlemanly. He confided to Richard his aspirations. He wished to learn French and proposed to join a Polytechnic Institute for the purpose. Also, he had thoughts of leaving home, and living in rooms, like Richard. He was now earning twenty-eight shillings a week; he intended to save money and to give up all intoxicants beyond half a pint of bitter a day. Richard responded willingly to his mood, and offered sound advice, which was listened to with deference. Then the talk, as often aforetime, drifted to the subject of women. It appeared that Jenkins had a desire to 'settle down' (he was twenty-one). He knew several fellows in the Walworth Road who had married on less than he was earning.

'What about Miss Roberts?' Richard questioned.

'Oh! She's off. She's a bit too old for me, you know. She must be twenty-six.'

'Look here, my boy,' said Richard, good-humouredly, 'I don't believe you ever had anything to do with her at all. It was nothing but boasting.'

'What will you bet I can't prove it to you?' Jenkins retorted, putting out his chin, an ominous gesture with him.

'I'll bet you half-a-crown — no, a shilling.'

'Done.'

Jenkins took a letter-case from his pocket, and handed Richard a midget photograph of Miss Roberts. Underneath it was her signature. 'Yours sincerely, Laura Roberts.'

Strange to say, the incident did not trouble Richard in the least.

He walked down to Victoria with Jenkins towards midnight, and on returning to his lodging, thought for the hundredth time how futile was his present mode of existence, how bare of all that makes life worth living. Of what avail to occupy pretty rooms, if one occupied them alone, coming into them at night to find them empty, leaving them in the morning without a word of farewell? In the waste of London, Laura Roberts made the one green spot. He had lost interest in his novel. On the other hand, his interest in the daily visit to the Crabtree was increasing.

As day succeeded day he fell into a practice of deliberately seeking out and magnifying the finer qualities in her nature, while ignoring those which were likely to offend him; indeed he refused to allow himself to be offended. He went so far as to retard his lunch-hour permanently, so that, the rush of customers being past, he should have better opportunity to talk to her without interruption. Then he timidly essayed the first accents of courtship, and finding his advances accepted, grew bolder. One Sunday morning he met her as she was coming out of the Wesleyan chapel at Munster Park; he said the encounter was due to accident. She introduced him to her relations, who were with her. Her father was a big, stout, dark man, dressed in black faced-cloth, with a heavy beard, huge chubby fingers, and jagged grey finger-nails. Her mother was a spare woman of sorrowful aspect, whose thin lips seldom moved; she held her hands in front of her, one on the top of the other. Her brother was a lank schoolboy, wearing a damaged mortar-board hat.

Shortly afterwards he called on her at Carteret Street. The schoolboy opened the door, and after inviting him as far as the lobby, vanished into a back room only to reappear and run upstairs. Richard heard his loud, agitated whisper: 'Laura, Laura, here's Mr Larch come to see you.'

They strolled to Wimbledon Common that night.

His entity seemed to have become dual. One part of him was willingly enslaved to an imperious, headstrong passion; the other stood calmly, cynically apart, and watched. There were hours when he could foresee the whole of his future life, and measure the bitter, ineffectual regret which he was laying up; hours when he admitted that his passion had been, as it were, artificially incited, and that there could be no hope of an enduring love. He liked Laura; she was a woman, a balm, a consolation. To all else he obstinately shut his eyes, and, casting away every consideration of prudence, hastened to involve himself more and more deeply. Swiftly, swiftly, the climax approached. He hailed it with a strange, affrighted joy.

XXXI

They were upon Chelsea Embankment in the late dusk of a Saturday evening in May. A warm and gentle wind stirred the budding trees to magic utterances. The long, straight line of serried lamps stretched away to an enchanted bridge which with twinkling lights hung poised over the misty river. The plash of an oar came languorously up from the water, and the voices of boys calling. At intervals, couples like themselves passed by, either silent or conversing in low tones that seemed to carry inner, inarticulate meanings. As for them, they were silent; he had not her arm, but they walked close together. He was deeply and indescribably moved; his heart beat heavily, and when he looked at her face in the gloom and saw that her eyes were liquid, it beat yet more heavily; then lay still.

'Let us sit down – shall we?' he said at length, and they turned to an empty bench under a tree. 'What is she thinking?' he wondered, and then the dominant feeling of the moment possessed him wholly. His ambitions floated out of sight and were forgotten. He remembered nothing except the girl by his side, whose maddening bosom rose and fell under his very gaze. At that moment she belonged to no class; had no virtues, no faults. All the inessentials of her being were stripped away, and she was merely a woman, divine, desired, necessary, waiting to be captured. She sat passive, expectant, the incarnation of the Feminine.

He took her hand, and felt it tremble. At the contact a thrill ran about him, and for a second a delicious faintness robbed him of all strength.

Then with inexplicable rapidity his mind went unerringly back to that train-journey to William's funeral. He saw the cottage in the fields, and the young mother, half robed and with sleep in her eyes, standing at the door. Exquisite vision!

He heard himself speaking, –

'Laura . . .'

The little hand gave a timorous encouragement.

'Laura . . . you are going to marry me.'

The intoxicating pressure of her lips on his was answer. Heedless of publicity, he crushed her against his breast, this palpitating creature with the serious face. Ah, she could love!

It was done. The great irretrievable moment had gone to join a million other moments of no significance. He felt triumphant, fiercely triumphant. His frightful solitude was at an end. One woman was his. A woman . . . his, his own!

See! A tear quivered in her eye. . . .

XXXII

Sunday was stiflingly hot. At Sloane Street the roof of every Putney omnibus was already laden with passengers, and Richard, on his way to Carteret Street to make the acquaintance of Laura's married sister, Milly Powell, her husband and young child, was forced at last to be content with a seat inside. The public houses were just closing for the afternoon, and the footpaths full of holiday-makers, with here and there a girl or a middle-aged man carrying a Bible. No vehicles were abroad except the omnibuses and an occasional hired carriage which passed by with a nonchalant, lazy air.

At the Redcliffe Arms there got in a little family party consisting of a stout, seemingly prosperous man, gruffly good-humoured, his wife, and a boy of about two years, whose puffy face was disfigured by large spectacles.

'Sit here, Milly, out of the sun,' the man said curtly.

Richard looked up at the sound of the name. The woman's likeness to Laura was unmistakable; beyond doubt she must be the sister of his betrothed. He examined her curiously. She was perhaps slightly under thirty, of a good height and well set, with a large head and a large, plain face. Her movements were clumsy. She appeared to be just upon the line which divides the matron from the young mother. In both her features and her attire there were faint reminders of girlish grace, or at least of the charm of the shy wife who nurses her first-born. Her complexion was clear and fresh, her ears small and delicately pink, her eyes cool grey. But one did not notice these beauties without careful inspection, while the heavy jaws, the lax eyelids, the flattened nose whose tilt unpleasantly revealed the nostrils, were obvious and repellent. She wore a black gown, which fitted badly, imparting an ungainliness probably foreign to her proper figure. Her broad hat of black straw, trimmed with poppies and cornflowers, was strikingly modish, and the veil, running at an angle from the extremity of the brim down to her chin, gave to her face a cloistered quality which had its own seductiveness. Her small hands were neatly gloved, and held a cheap, effective parasol. The woman's normal expression was one of cow-like vacancy, but now and then her eyes would light up as she spoke to the child, gently restraining it, reassuring it, rallying it with simple banter. She was still in love with her husband; frequently she glanced at him with furtive wistfulness. She was able to enjoy the summer weather. She was not quite dead to the common phenomena of the roadside. But the last resistances of departing youthfulness and vivacity against the narcotic of a dull, unlovely domesticity were taking place. In a year or two she would be the typical matron of the lower middle-class.

When Richard had made these observations, he reflected: 'Laura will be like that – soon.' Mentally he compared the two faces, and he could, as it were, see Laura's changing. . . .

Then followed a reverie which embraced the whole of his past life. He recognised that, while he bore all the aspect of prosperity, he had failed. Why had nature deprived him of strength of purpose? Why could not he, like other men, bend circumstances to his own ends? He sought for a reason, and he found it in his father, that mysterious, dead transmitter of traits, of whom he knew so little, and on whose name lay a blot of some kind which was hidden from him. He had been born in the shadow, and after a fitful struggle towards emergence, into the shadow he must again retire. Fate was his enemy. Mary had died; Mary would have helped him to be strong. Mr Aked had died; Mr Aked's inspiring influence would have incited and guided his efforts. Adeline had abandoned him to a fatal loneliness.

He knew well that he would make no further attempt to write. Laura was not even aware that he had had ambitions in that direction. He had never told her, because she would not have understood. She worshipped him, he felt sure, and at times he had a great tenderness for her; but it would be impossible to write in the suburban doll's-house which was to be theirs. No! In future he would be simply the suburban husband – dutiful towards his employers, upon whose grace he would be doubly dependent; keeping his house in repair; pottering in the garden; taking his wife out for a walk, or occasionally to the theatre; and saving as much as he could. He would be good to his wife – she was his. He wanted to get married at once. He wanted to be master of his own dwelling. He wanted to have Laura's kiss when he went out of a morning to earn the bread-and-cheese. He wanted to see her figure at the door when he returned at night. He wanted to share with her the placid, domestic evening. He wanted to tease her, and to get his ears boxed and be called a great silly. He wanted to creep into the kitchen and surprise her with a pinch of the cheek as she bent over the range. He wanted to whisk her up in his arms, carry her from one room to another, and set her down breathless in a chair. . . . Ah! Let it be soon. And as for the more distant future, he would not look at that. He would keep his eyes on the immediate foreground, and be happy while he could. After all, perhaps things had been ordered for the best; perhaps he had no genuine talent for writing. And yet at that moment he was conscious that he possessed the incommunicable imaginative insights of the author. . . . But it was done with now.

The conductor called out their destination, and as Laura's sister gathered the child in her arms he sprang out and hurried down Carteret Street in order to reach the house first and so avoid a meeting on the doorstep. He heard the trot of the child behind him. Children . . . Perhaps a child of his might give sign of literary ability. If so – and surely these instincts descended, were not lost – how he would foster and encourage it!

WHOM GOD HATH JOINED

ARNOLD BENNETT

In *Whom God Hath Joined*, Bennett was on his home ground of the Five Towns. With great sympathy and realism he tells the story of two domestic tragedies which, in their different ways, lead to the divorce court.

Phyllis Ridware should have married her husband's friend and by so doing both she and Lawrence would have been spared the fate that was to overwhelm them. On discovering that the man to whom she had once been engaged is suffering from a fatal illness, Phyllis becomes his lover, begins to hate her husband and is led inexorably towards the Law Courts. Lawrence Ridware, incidentally, is a clerk in the firm of that prominent Five Towns solicitor Charles Fearns. Now Charlie is a philanderer. He seduces his children's French governess and is found out. The scenes in court are both moving and dramatic and show Bennett at his best.

HELEN WITH THE HIGH HAND

ARNOLD BENNETT

It is difficult to say who is the more delightful in this charming domestic comedy: James Ollerenshaw or high-handed Helen who arrives to disturb his miserly, measured existence.

When Helen Rathbone met her estranged step-uncle James on a park bench in one of the Five Towns, no citizen of this provincial manufacturing region could have guessed what a turn events would take, least of all the two protagonists. Helen was quite convinced she could change James Ollerenshaw for the better, while he was equally determined that she should not. From that moment their lives were inextricably bound together and would affect many more inside and outside their circle.

THE MATADOR OF
THE FIVE TOWNS

ARNOLD BENNETT

When Mr Loring, a visitor from London, is forced upon the hospitality of Dr Stirling, he becomes caught up in a sequence of totally unexpected events, and ends up experiencing the frenzied atmosphere of a football match in which Jos Myatt, 'The Matador of the Five Towns', is playing. But when the finest full-back in the league arrives at the doctor's house, events become more sombre . . .

Will Arthur Cotterill make it to London in time for his appointment? He doesn't think so when he wakes up, believing he has twenty minutes to get to the station. Fortunately his brother, Simeon, had put the clock on and disaster is averted. But this is only the first of many occasions on which Arthur's heart is set racing. 'Catching the Train' is Arnold Bennett at his most entertaining.

Both tragic and humourous, the stories in *The Matador of the Five Towns* chronicle events in the everyday lives of the Potteries' citizens.

THE PRETTY LADY

ARNOLD BENNETT

The coincidence frightened her, but it also delighted her . . . 'Was it not astounding that on one night of all nights he should have been at the Marigny? Was it not still more astounding that on one night of all nights he should have been in the Promenade in Leicester Square? . . . The affair was ordained from the beginning of time . . .'

So starts a relationship which explores two contrasting characters and their incompatible approaches to life. A young French courtesan and a respectable, middle-aged Englishman pursue their lives against a back-drop of London, war committees and class-consciousness at the outbreak of the First World War.

The scene is set for another classic Arnold Bennett novel.